THE TRAIL TO REBELLION

PLAINSMAN WESTERN SERIES BOOK SIX

B.N. RUNDELL

WOLFPACK
PUBLISHING
— EST 2013 —

The Trail to Rebellion
Paperback Edition
© Copyright 2022 B.N. Rundell

Wolfpack Publishing
5130 S. Fort Apache Rd. 215-380
Las Vegas, NV 89148

wolfpackpublishing.com

Paperback ISBN 978-1-63977-920-8
Large Print Hardcover ISBN 978-1-63977-921-5
eBook ISBN 978-1-63977-919-2

To the many readers that have given their time and treasure to participate in these stories. Without you, all the effort of the publisher, the staff, and more would be to no avail. Not to mention the hours spent staring at a computer screen that sits quietly, waiting for my fingers to start talking. You are the best! Without you, there would be no books, not just those penned by me, but every author that has given their time, talent, and imagination to provide entertainment, encouragement, and maybe a little excitement. Just knowing you are there, before these pages, reading what has been written, gives me and every other author a special joy. And for that, I thank each and every one of you!

THE TRAIL TO REBELLION

1 / DISCOVERY

The two old timers sat near the pot belly stove taking in the early activity in Morgan's Emporium. The general store was the oldest established business in the new settlement called Cañon City. The town was all of four years old on this spring morning of 1864 and had seen its ups and downs. Shortly after founding it boasted a population over seven hundred, but with the war and the recruitment efforts of the Union, the area had raised two regiments of the Second Infantry of Colorado Volunteers that had recently been assigned and marched out to Fort Garland. Now the town was showing early signs of a ghost town, the only residents being old men and women, left behind wives and rambunctious children.

"I'm tellin' ya, Homer. If'n them rebels hadn't left when they did, we'd hadta get the rest o' the ol' timers together an' run 'em out! They smelled like trouble!" declared the whiskery face with tobacco stains running from both corners of his toothless mouth. His galluses were straining over his paunch and pulling at his often patched and faded canvas britches. He leaned both hands on his walking stick as he leaned closer to the stove, giving the tobacco another chaw.

"Oh pshaw! Lucius, just cuz they was wearin' grey don't mean they was huntin' trouble! You was just wishin' you could get back in the fight, 'sides the last time you fired that ol' blunderbuss was to celebrate your birthday! An' then you couldn't recollect how old you was!"

"I ain't so old I don't remember when I was in the fight! I'll have you know I was with both Robert E. Lee and Ulysses S. Grant when we fought together down thar in Chapultepec, just outside o' Mexico City durin' that dust up with Mexico back in 1846!"

"I heerd you tell that before, an' I still don't believe it!"

"I'm tellin' you it's the gospel! Why, after ol' Lee got wounded, Grant had us fellers break down a howitzer and drag it up in the church steeple. We done went an' put it back t'gether an' bombarded the dickens outta them Mez'cans! Ol' Grant got promoted to Captain after that, an' we'uns didn't even get extry beans!"

Reuben had turned to look at the old timers, leaning back against the counter and smiling while the storekeeper filled his order. His wife, Elly, and their friend, Estrella, waited outside with the horses while Reuben was stocking up on supplies. He grinned at the conversation, then stepped closer and asked, "So gentlemen, tell me 'bout those fellas you thought were confederates."

Homer nodded to Lucius, "I din't think they was, but that ol' coot did! Let him tell ya." The two men could have passed for brothers, both were probably in the upper reaches of their sixties if not more and were attired in faded and patched canvas britches held up by galluses. Homer wore a tattered linsey Woolsey shirt that at one time appeared to be blue, but now favored grey, while Lucius sported a checkered red and white store-bought cotton shirt that had almost as many tobacco stains as checks.

Lucius turned to face Reuben, looking him up and down, and asked, "Ain't them uniform britches? But they looks like they was green!" he lifted his eyes with eyebrows raised to wait for Reuben's answer.

Reuben grinned, glancing down at his woolen britches, "You've got a good eye! Yup, they are uniform britches and they're green cuz that's what those of us in Berdan's sharpshooters wore, everything was green."

"Butchu ain't in it no more?" quizzed Lucius.

"No, took a little too much lead, but I had served my hitch and was gettin' out anyway."

Lucius and Homer gave Reuben the once over, eyeing the tall, broad-shouldered man with long blonde hair that hung just short of his shoulders. The flat-brimmed felt hat was pushed back on his head to reveal a strong chiseled face, broad forehead, high cheek bones, and dark eyes that showed wisdom and mischief. The old men had heard of Berdan's Sharpshooters and knew they were a cut above the rest of the Union soldiers. They were all exceptional marksmen and good woodsmen and had done more than their share of fighting in the early stages of the war and the looks of this man told the story well.

"You passin' thru or are you gonna stay a spell?" asked Homer, leaning back a little and scooting a little closer to the stove.

"Just passin' through. Got a cabin back up in the Wet Mountain valley and takin' a ride to South Park. Curious about them fellas you spoke of, the ones wearin' grey?" asked Reuben, glancing back to the storekeeper still busy at his task.

Lucius scooted to the edge of his seat, "Now this is how I see it. Weren't more'n a week ago, an' they was Confederates alright, 'though their uniforms were a little mixed up an' all, but they looked to their leader and did what he said. Some of 'em had those light blue britches with a yeller stripe, others had a combination of floppy hat, kinda like yourn, and that butternut and grey on their jackets. Didn't none of 'em wear stripes an' such, but you could tell by their manner which ones was officers and not. There was 'bout fifteen or so, give or take, and when they came through, their horses were a mite weary, but they kept on goin'. Reckon they didn't get too fer 'fore they camped. But from what me'n Homer heard, I think they was goin' to South Park too."

"What kind of weapons did they have?"

"Now that's what convinced me they was sojers. Ever one of 'em had Springfields. You know those what use them thar paper caw'tridges? Some of 'em had those Square D handled Bowie knives, too. Couple of 'em had them yeller sashes." He paused, looked up at Reuben as he cocked his head to the side, then continued, "If'n you was to take count of what any o' the fellers here'bouts had, wouldn't be two or three of 'em have Springfields, and they would be discharged so'jers, just like you! You carry a Springfield?"

Reuben grinned, dropped his head and looked back up to the men, "No. The sharpshooters favored the Sharps, that's what I carry. Did you hear anything else from those men?"

Homer looked at Lucius and back at Reuben, shaking his head as he answered, "Nuthin' worth repeatin'!" He paused, glanced to Lucius before asking, "You goin' to look fer gold like the rest o' them fools?"

Reuben couldn't help but chuckle at the question,

shook his head and answered, "Nope! I had enough diggin' in the dirt on my father's farm, and decided I was not cut out for that."

"Wal, you're smarter'n you look then!" answered Homer, cackling as he slapped Lucius' knee, prompting his friend to add his toothless giggle to the fray.

The storekeeper pushed the stack of goods forward, bumping Reuben and causing him to turn around. "That'll be twelve an' a half dollars."

Reuben nodded, fished out a ten-dollar gold eagle and a five-dollar half eagle and put them on the counter. The storekeeper's eyes flared, his eyebrows raised, and he looked up at Reuben with a broad smile, "We sure don't see these very often!" as he slid them into his hand. He counted out the change with the more common copper, nickel, and silver smaller coins, and handed them to Reuben. He scooped up an armload and started for the door, the storekeeper following with his own armload.

"Well, it's about time! I was about to come in after you!" declared a smiling Elly. The petite blonde woman was Reuben's wife of a little more than a year. They met when Elly, or Eleanor, and her family was traveling west with a Mormon wagon train that Reuben helped guide through the prairies of Nebraska territory. She had sided Reuben in fights against the Pawnee, Sioux, and Cheyenne as well as their little set to with the Confederates that were trying to highjack the Overland stage line. Both Reuben and Elly, at the request of Ben Holladay, had been appointed Deputy Marshals by the new governor of Colorado territory after they rounded up some outlaws and returned the gold shipment.

They had worked with the Union Cavalry to ensure the rebels failed in taking one of the largest gold shipments by the Overland Stage and Ben Holladay had shown his appreciation with a handsome reward and encouraged the governor to put the two to work permanently. Now they were bound for South Park and another assignment from the governor.

Standing beside Elly was a smiling Estrella Esquibel, a young Mexican woman who had been a captive of the Apache until Reuben traded a pair of rifles for her and a couple horses. But when they traveled south to return her to her father, his new bride of Comanche lineage was less than welcoming, and everyone agreed it would be best for Estrella to stay with Reuben and Elly. After spending the winter in the mountain cabin, the expanded family was now bound for the high plains of South Park, the middle of the Pike's Peak Gold Rush.

They worked together to load the rest of the supplies. With two pack horses and one pack mule, all outfitted with pack saddles, panniers and parfleches, there was ample space for all the new supplies which included ammunition for the three Henry rifles, paper cartridges for Reuben's Sharps, paper cartridges for Reuben's Remington Army pistol, powder, and lead for Elly's .36 caliber Colt Pocket revolver. Other supplies included the staples of flour, sugar, cornmeal, bacon, and a few cans of peaches. It was late afternoon when the three rode from the supply town of Cañon City, going west into the foothills where they would take the supply road that turned north to South Park.

2 / FOOTHILLS

R euben wanted to put some distance between them and the town before dark settled over the foothills. After leaving the burg, the trail sided the long ridge of hogbacks then turned west to work its way through the scattered piñon and juniper covered hills. As they crested the hills and took to the flats, the sun was lowering in the west and the golden orb made them duck their heads or lift their hands to shade their eyes as the trail took them straight into the golden sunset. As the bright sun began to tuck itself away beyond the rugged horizon, colors splashed across the sky, every wisp of a cloud latching onto the colors to strut across the heavens and share the gold with the empty sky by bouncing long lances of orange and gold across the foothills, making the range appear to be dipped in the pale paint of elapsed time.

The trail bent to the north and Reuben spotted a break in the hills where a small spring fed stream fought its way to the valley bottom to add its meager offering to the headwaters of Currant Creek. He followed the rimrock lined hillside that lay on the west edge of the creek, until they approached the spring. He nodded to the women, motioned to the flat grass covered area that was sided by the tall rimrock cliffs on the west, the lower bank of the canyon on the east and ample cover of juniper near the water. Reuben stepped down, led Blue and the mule to the water, followed by the women leading their horses and pack animals. Elly and Estrella dropped the leads to their animals and started gathering some firewood to start the cookfire while Reuben tended to the horses. He stripped the gear from each one, rubbed it down with a hand full of dry grass, and picketed each one within reach of grass and water.

He had stacked the packsaddles and panniers to one side, within easy reach of the women, took the bedrolls to the shade of the junipers, then with rifle slung over one shoulder, his small haversack on the other, he motioned to Bear, their big black dog that looked more like a wolf than a dog that was found at a campsite used by many wagon trains, apparently left behind by some previous train, and with a nod to the women, started up the narrow trail that would take him atop the rimrock ridge and afford him a view of their surroundings in the fading light of dusk. Once atop the ridge, he walked a little further to the north for a higher point of view. He found a big rock beside a cluster of piñons and took a seat, withdrawing the binoculars for a scan of the territory.

They were surrounded by the many foothills of the lower Rockies. Behind them lay the gorge of the Arkansas River, but before them were the hills that lay south of the massive South Park, the scene of the many mines and diggings of the Gold Rush. He could see the break in the hills that held the trail they would travel on the morrow, and the entire area was showing the green-up of spring. The pale green of buffalo grass, bunch grass and some blue gramma covered the flat lands and was interspersed with the juniper, piñon, and cedar. The last time they traveled through this area, the only color was the muted greens of the trees and a lot of brown and tan of drought burnt grasses. But the green of spring held promise of a better year.

Although it had been about a week since the supposed band of Confederates passed, there were still signs of the sizable groups passing. Reuben and his women had passed a campsite that was devoid of graze and covered with hoof prints and droppings of many horses that Reuben supposed had been one of their campsites. But there was nothing showing as far as he could see of any other living thing apart from a few deer that were tiptoeing their way to their evening water. Satisfied, he rose to start back to camp but paused when Bear stopped, dropping his head low and letting a deep growl rumble from his chest. Reuben slipped the Sharps from his shoulder, bringing it across his chest and earing back the hammer to place a cap on the nipple. With the hammer at half-cock, he glimpsed the narrow wisp of the campfire as it snaked its way into the silent and still sky. Nothing appeared to be amiss as Bear padded beside him to slowly approach the camp from cover. Two figures sat side by side, apparently a man and a woman, their backs to the trees as Reuben and Bear padded silently through the trees to approach the camp like the wisp of the morning, low, slow, and silent.

Elly and Estrella worked well together, and the smell of a fine meal caught Reuben's attention. The two women were relaxed and talking with the visitors and no weapons were within sight, but caution was his habit and he stepped from behind the trees, the rifle held low across his chest, his thumb on the hammer, ready to bring it to full cock and fire. He was surprised to see they had company as there had been no sign of any others save the Confederates and it was immediately obvious these were not a part of the rebel band.

The broad back of the man showed muscles that were evidence of much hard, back breaking labor, but the single strap from the coveralls stretched over a broad shoulder and a deep basso profundo voice resonated whenever he spoke. Reuben guessed the man to be close to six feet tall but built like a bull or a grizzly. The woman was petite in comparison to the man and leaned against the man reminding Reuben of a mother hen sheltering her lone chick, his big arm around her waist to hold her close and protected.

Reuben and Bear stood in the shadows, quietly listening, and watching, until Elly looked up, smiled, and announced, "Why, here's my Reuben now!" and motioned him to come into the camp.

Reuben stepped forward, not lowering his rifle, and looked at the two visitors. They were coloreds and it was not common to see them in this part of the country. Elly smiled, nodded to the visitors and said, "Reuben, this is Levi and Precious Green! They saw us when we came to camp and thought they would visit. Isn't that nice?"

Reuben nodded, quickly noticed there were no weapons, at least not in sight, and stepped forward, extending his hand to shake and introduce himself, "Pleased to meet'chu! I'm Reuben," dropped his eyes to Bear and motioned him close, "And this is Bear."

The big dog stepped forward slowly, sniffing and looking at both visitors, then pushed closer and lay his chin on Levi's knee. The man grinned and reached out to ruffle Bear's scruff and rub behind his ears, glancing at his woman as she did the same. Reuben looked around, and back to the visitors, "No horses?"

"Oh, we got us a mule back in the trees yonder, but not much else," rumbled the big man, nodding and glancing around a little nervously. "We been travelin' for several weeks now and we's 'bout worn out!"

"Where 'bouts you hail from?" asked Reuben, taking a seat on the big rock nearby. He leaned the Sharps against the stone and slipped the haversack from his shoulder to set it nearby.

The big man frowned, glanced to his woman and back to Reuben, "Back east a ways."

"Seems like everybody comes from back east a ways. My childhood home was Michigan and Elly's was Missouri or someplace like that. Now, Estrella there, she's from down in Mexico territory, when she's not gadding about that is." He looked at the girl who shook her head, laughing at Reuben's remark and glancing to the visitors.

"What he means is, whenever I'm not a captive of the Apache or the Comanche or whoever decides they need somebody to wait on 'em hand and foot, like Reuben there!" Elly, Reuben, and Estrella chuckled at the retort and glanced to their visitors who were frowning.

Levi looked from under his heavy brow at Reuben as he moved his arm from behind Precious and placed his hand on her knee. "Is she your captive, your slave?" he growled.

Reuben shook his head, grinning but understanding

11

the concern of the big man and said, "If anybody's a slave around here, it's me! Those two women keep me hoppin' all the time! No, she's not a slave, although the Apache and Comanche tried to make her one, but I think they were glad to be rid of her cuz' she's a handful!" he chuckled as he looked at the smiling girl.

Reuben looked to Levi and said, "My friend, we don't hold with slavery, and besides, here in the territory, slavery is illegal. But that doesn't stop some slave catchers from trying to capture what they consider to be runaways or anyone they can claim to be runaways." He paused, leaned forward with elbows on his knees as he looked at Levi, "So, if you're a runaway, here in the territory, it doesn't matter, and as far as we're concerned, you're just as free as any of us. Besides, a little matter called the *Emancipation Proclamation* said you are a free man and free woman anyway, and anybody that says different, will have to deal with me," as he said the last, he slipped the Deputy Marshal badge from his jacket pocket and held it in his hand beside his leg for both visitors to see. The firelight bounced off the badge, making it shine as if it were a bright light, and the reflected light bounced off the dark skin of Levi but clearly showed a broad smile of white teeth and dimpled cheeks.

"So! Enough talk about that! Let's eat!" declared Elly, motioning to the pans full of goodness. Reuben snatched up the coffee pot and poured coffee all around as each one filled their tin plates from the big pot of stew and grabbed a cornmeal biscuit. As they sat back to enjoy the food, Elly scooted close to Reuben, lay her head on his shoulder, and whispered, "It's always amazing to me how the good Lord brings people to us that need help or protection. Oh, and don't forget, you're *my* protector too!"

"Uh, I thought it was the other way 'round. Aren't you *my* protector?" replied a grinning Reuben. But Bear pushed himself against their legs as if to correct them both as to who was the real protector.

3 / TRAVELERS

Now there were five. The two visitors, Levi and Precious, had accepted Reuben's offer to ride with them. He offered them the bay packhorse to ride, letting their mule fill in as a pack animal. "Yes'r, ol' Meg would let us ride a little, but after 'while, she gets plumb onery and makes us walk. We was getting mighty tired o' walkin' but din't have no choice," explained Levi, shaking his head in consternation.

Reuben grinned, nodded to their mule, "I've known some mules that are good riders, but like you say, some of 'em can be ornery as the day is long and there's no sense in arguing with the original stubborn animal. Sometimes I think the good Lord made them just to teach us patience!"

Levi chuckled, "I'se reckon you right 'bout dat. Meg was a good 'un in the field, weren't no plow she couldn't pull through the rockiest ground, an' she'd lean into that collar and rip the groun' up! But if'n she got tired, you could put a couple horns o' black powder under her an' set it off and she still wouldn't move, no sir."

Shortly after leaving camp at first light, the trail bent

to the west away from the trickle of a creek and took to the flats for easy going. After riding the dry lowland, it crossed a dry wash that had seen many a runoff and bent to the north to cut through the timbered but lower foothills. After close to three miles, they struck Currant Creek that now carried a bit more water, fed by the spring runoff of the surrounding hills, and stayed on the trail that sided the creek as it cut its way through the foothills. They had ridden about a dozen miles, maybe a little further, when they came to a fork in the trails, but the one on the right showed both sign of wagons, probably freighters, and the fresher sign of the band of Confederates. He motioned everyone to a grassy flat beside the creek where a break in the willows showed a well-traveled game trail that brought the animals to water.

Reuben stepped down beside Blue, let him take his long drink, then loosened the girth and ground tied him beside the grass. The others did the same and Elly led the ladies to gather the morning's leftovers and a pan to begin preparing a mid-day meal. Reuben glanced to Levi, "I'm goin' up that hill yonder to have a look-see around us, if you wanna come?"

"Yessuh, shore do. I need to stretch these legs. Ain't used to ridin' so fer wit'out a break." He arched his back, his hands on his hips and stretched out as best he could. As Reuben turned, he tossed the Henry rifle to Levi, which the man adroitly caught, and asked, "You know how to use that?"

Levi looked at it as he turned it over in his hands, examining the workmanship and the feel of the weapon. He looked up at Reuben, "I'se never used one like this, but I reckon it ain't too hard."

"Just jack a round into the chamber with that lever,"

started Reuben, nodding to the rifle, "lift it, sight down the barrel, and pull the trigger. It holds fourteen shells, loaded through that notch in the side of the receiver." Levi nodded as Reuben stepped out, Bear was beside him and Levi quickly followed. Reuben nodded and waved to Elly, who nodded in return, knowing the habit of her husband to always take to high ground to survey the countryside around, before settling into any camp, even a short stop like nooning.

It was only about a hundred yards as they crossed a slight rise, walked through the sandy wash, and climbed the piñon freckled hillside to reach the point Reuben chose for his scan of the country. Atop the knob of the hill, he seated himself in the shade of a tall juniper and withdrew his binoculars for his search. With elbows on knees, he searched the trail before them, made a quick scan behind them, and a general look around the surrounding hills. Satisfied, he offered the binoculars to Levi, "Have a look. I didn't see anything interesting."

Levi grinned, lifted the glasses for his own scan and moved about, enjoying the view like he had never seen before. He lowered the glasses to hand them to Reuben and asked, "You said you was goin' into the South Park. What'chu gonna do?"

"Well, the governor said there were several stage holdups that took some of the gold shipments bound for the east and he thinks we might be able to find those that have done that."

Levi nodded, looking around and thinking. Reuben saw the expression of wonder on the man's face and asked, "What're your plans?"

"Dunno. Reckon I needs to find work some'eres. Don't rightly know what. But me'n the missus need a place to live and money for food an' such."

"There are several businesses in the towns, stores, hotels, taverns, and such. Many of them could use help, since most men are searching for gold and don't want to be tied down with a regular job. And there are some of the mines that need miners, both experienced and inexperienced."

"Does you know many folks aroun' those places?" asked Levi, a hopeful look on his face.

"Not very many. We weren't here long enough to get acquainted with many people, but I'll be glad to put in a good word for you, if you'd like."

Levi frowned as he looked at Reuben, "But you don't know me, why'd you want to do that?"

Reuben grinned, slipping the field glasses back in the case, and looked up at the man, "Levi, I'm a pretty good judge of character and I think you're a good man that would be willing to work hard and take care of his family. I'd be happy to do whatever I could to help you get settled." He paused, looking around, "When we were here before, finding a place to live wasn't all that difficult. There have been several prospectors that went bust and walked away from their diggings and their cabins. You might be able to find one that would suit the two of you just fine."

"You mean it'd be empty and just waitin' for somebody to take it?" asked Levi, a little incredulous at the thought.

"That's right. Most of 'em aren't all that great, but at least it could be a start for you."

"Well, if that don't beat all," said Levi, shaking his head in wonder.

Reuben led the way as they started back down the hill, following a bit of a game trail where deer had traveled to and from the creek. Levi asked as they walked,

"These fellas lookin' fer gold, how do they know where to look?"

Reuben chuckled, "Truth be told, most of 'em don't know where to look. But gold is usually found in one of two places, wherever there's a lot of quartz, and in streams that have washed over gold deposits and carried it with the current. Gold is heavy and gathers in the bottom of riffles and such, so many men do what they call panning. Using a flat bottom pan to scoop up the sand, wash it around and the motion leaves the gold in the bottom while the lightweight sand and such wash out. There are other ways, of course, rocker boxes, sluice boxes, and such, but doesn't matter the means, it matters if there's gold.

"Those that don't get it from the stream, find deposits in veins among the quartz and do what they call hard-rock mining, blasting it out of the hard rock, breaking up the rock and getting to the gold. That's the hard way, but if there's gold, that way usually pays off better."

"Why don't you go for gold like them others?" asked Levi.

Reuben chuckled, "Well, Levi, most of those fellas that look for it, find nothing but hardship and empty pockets. But as far as I'm concerned, I've never been one to go chasing after rainbows and riches. I've got most everything I've ever wanted," nodding toward Elly and smiling. They were nearing the camp and the women looked up and waved just as Reuben finished talking.

Levi looked at the man, nodded, "Yessuh, I understand," and smiled toward Precious.

The travel had been easy, and the horses were still fresh, so the noon break was brief, and they were soon back on the trail. Although Reuben and Elly had traveled this way before, when they left South Park bound for the future site of their cabin, that was in the fall, and spring-time going the opposite direction, everything looked different. They took the trail that separated from Currant Creek, following a wide draw that carried the freighter road. The foothills shouldered in from the west, low foothills stretched to the east and the trail pointed basically north.

Soon the trail dropped down to cross over and side Currant Creek once again. As they followed it through the timbered foothills, several patches of aspen stood tall on their white barked trunks and waved their light green leaves at the passersby. It was a pleasant spring day, and the sun was lowering off their left shoulder. They had covered about another dozen miles when Reuben pointed Blue away from the trail into an aspen clad arroyo to make camp for the night. A spring fed creek sided the grassy flat and the camp was soon made comfortable and cozy by the women, with the men taking to the nearby hilltop for one last look around.

4 / PARK

The bald knob was about three hundred feet higher than their camp in the bottom of the aspen rich arroyo, but the nearby hills rose much higher, limiting Reuben's view of the valley. The long timbered ridge of the shadowed mountain masked the slow rising sun, but the break at the end of the big ridge told of the north by northwest trail that pointed to Fairplay and Buckskin further upstream on the South Platte River. What had been a very visible trail of the band of Confederates had faded, the wind of the high flatland erasing any sign of passing, but Reuben guessed them to be focused on the gold fields and that would mean they were bound toward the boom towns of Buckskin, Tarryall, and Fairplay.

As he scanned the valley in the dim light of early morning, he remembered the words of the telegram from the governor, *Confederate rebels causing trouble with the stage lines* ... He knew that meant there were those that used the colors of the South to rob the stages of gold bound for the Union forces. Not all the highwaymen were Southern sympathizers and not all the sympathizers were sending their ill-gotten gains to the Confederacy, if *any* were. *But all that trouble started well before this bunch came north, that is, unless these are some of the same bunch.* He saw nothing alarming, several deer coming for their morning water and graze, a small bunch of Pronghorns doing the same, and the ever-present coyotes looking for easy prey for their meal.

He stood and started back to the camp, Bear at his side, anxious for his morning coffee and to get an early start on their travels. It would still be about two days travel to Fairplay and even further to Buckskin, but that was where he would find the latest news on any robberies and any possible supporters of the Confederacy cause.

Everyone was up and about, the women busy with fixing the first meal of the day and Levi rigging the horses with saddles and packs. Reuben noticed the big man lifting the hooves of each of the animals, cleaning several and checking the condition of each one. He walked closer, "You have a good touch with the animals, it appears you've been doin' that a long time," suggested Reuben, wanting to learn more about their new traveling companions.

"Yassuh, done it a bit. Been a smithy a few years, but most towns already have one an' I ain't got the money to get the tools I need. Reckon I'll hafta do sumpin' else 'fore I can get back to it," replied Levi, dropping the hoof of the palomino claimed by Estrella. "You've got yoursef' some mighty fine animals here," he added, stroking the neck of the yellow horse, glancing to Reuben as he spoke.

"That one," started Reuben, nodding to the palomino, "I traded from the Arapaho in the same deal that freed

Estrella. That other palomino we garnered when we repelled an attack by some Comanche."

Levi frowned, "You mean you been with all them Injuns, tradin' and fightin' and you still got'chur hair? I thought all them wild Injuns scalped folks!"

Reuben grinned, shaking his head, "Levi, there's always good and bad among any people, no matter the color of their skin. We've been friends with the Arapaho, the Mouache Ute, and others. Haven't been too friendly with the Comanche, though."

The men walked side by side as they returned to the cookfire for the first meal of the day and Levi looked to Reuben, "Is you a Christian, Mr. Reuben?"

Reuben grinned, "It's not *Mister*, it's just Reuben, and yes, I am a Christian, and so is Elly and Estrella. And by Christian, I mean we have each received Jesus Christ as our Savior. Is that what you mean when you say *Christian?*"

"Yassuh, that's zactly what I means," answered Levi, letting a broad grin split his face and showcase his white teeth that were matched by the whites of his eyes as he looked to his woman, Precious.

"Then Levi, how about you asking for the Lord's blessing for our food and our day's travels?" suggested Reuben.

"Yassuh," responded Levi, reaching for the hand of his wife who took Elly's in turn as did Estrella and Reuben. The big man let his thunderous voice roll through the aspen, seeking the Lord's attention to his prayer and asked for His blessings on the meal and the day and especially on their new friends. He spoke as if the Lord himself was standing by the trees, watching and listening, and his confidence and friendly manner made everyone else believe the Savior was smiling down on the big man. When Levi said "Amen" the others echoed his word and dropped their hands as they looked from one to the other, smiling.

They were soon on the trail, Reuben leading the way with Bear out in front, who often turned to look over his shoulder to be certain the others were following. The animals were fresh and eager for the trail, stepping out lively and lifting their hooves high, yet every drop of a hoof lifted a little cloud of dust, and the animals were soon showing the rigors of the trail.

They passed the long timbered ridge as the ridge top trees lifted spiney fingers to scratch at the rising sun, but the blazing light soon lifted above the treetops and bent golden rays to warm the backs of the band of travelers. It was a little over an hour since they started and the trail dipped into a vale that held a trickle of a stream carrying ice cold mountain water, prompting them to let the horses have a quick drink before continuing. With Blue's nose in the water, Reuben looked up and down the stream, and noticed some sign he thought was from the band of rebels. He quickly scanned the hills before them, saw nothing of concern and lifted Blue's head to return to the trail.

Reuben was remembering this country as they continued north. This was the area where he and the other members of the posse from Buckskin had tracked the Espinoza brothers. As the country flattened and the trail widened, Elly had moved up beside him and he turned to her, pointing to the lone timbered hill on their left, "That's where the posse met up with us as we were chasing the Espinoza brothers." He stood in his stirrups and pointed to the bigger mountain they had passed on their right, "We ended up trackin' 'em back over that-away." He turned back around in his seat, nodded to the north, "We'll hit the South Platte 'bout mid-day. Good place to stop for noonin'."

They made another ten miles and drew up on the bank of the South Platte. At its deepest, the river was no more than three feet deep, but mostly the slow-moving stream that twisted its way through the flats was about two feet deep and had a gravelly bottom. Big trout could be seen riding the current, waiting for the water to carry their food to them as they lazed in the cold water. Reuben saw several trout scatter as he led the way across the river and suggested to Elly, "If you'd like, I could try to get us some fish for dinner."

"That would be a pleasant change. I've eaten so much deer meat I was beginning to think I was growing antlers!" she smiled as she giggled while she watched her man twist in his saddle to look at her.

"Better not! Only bucks have antlers, and you'd look a mite silly sproutin' horns!" answered Reuben.

"Then catch us some nice trout!" she admonished as they came from the water.

They hurriedly made their mid-day camp, stripping the animals of their gear so they could roll, and the men could give them a rub down. Reuben recruited Levi to join him on their fishing expedition and the men soon left the women to their ways, knowing the ladies, led by Elly, would search the riverbanks for any edibles to add to the meal. Elly had already promised some fresh cattail sprouts, some onions, and maybe some timpsila.

Levi used the spade to turn some sod for some fresh worms while Reuben snatched at some grasshoppers and the men soon had ample bait for their fishing. With hooks and line in hand, they cut some willows and soon had their gear complete, and each found a deep hole in the bend of the river to drop in their hooks. They were about ten yards apart and each sat back from the bank, reclining in the tall grass and closing their eyes to the sun.

Levi had landed his sixth big trout, three were rainbows, two were cutthroat, and one was a golden, when Reuben looked over and said, "Hey, leave some for me!" just as his willow dipped again and he started bringing in his fourth. Levi was baiting his hook when he heard the bray of a mule, the long bray and short bursts that followed. Frowning he stood and looked upstream toward the camp where the animals were tethered, but from what he could see all the horses and the two mules were still at the camp. He hollered to Reuben, "Did you hear that mule?"

Reuben was standing and looking around also, "Yeah! But I thought it came from that way," pointing to the bluffs beyond the willows. As he spoke, a lone mule, harness dragging, showed himself above the willows as he brayed again. He had apparently smelled the horses and mules and was searching for them. Reuben frowned, knowing a harnessed mule meant someone was around and probably in trouble. He snatched up his trout and started back to the camp at a trot, motioning to Levi to follow. As he quickened his pace, he thought *I know we're near the Hartsel ranch, but not much else is around here. The road yonder is a freight road, maybe some freighter had a problem.* Then the thought of the rebels came to mind, and he shook his head, knowing there was trouble nearby.

5 / STAGE

Reuben and Levi hurriedly saddled the horses, Levi taking the palomino that had previously been used as a pack horse and they were soon beside the stray mule. It was evident the animal was used to people and horses as he came close, sniffing and moving about as Reuben leaned down and grabbed the long rein that trailed beside the animal. He looked at the harness and the broken single tree that bounced off the hind hocks of the mule and with a glance to Levi, "I think this mule is from a freighter or stage." He tossed the long rein to Levi, "You take him back to camp, I'll start back tracking him and you can follow."

With a nod, Levi swung the palomino around and started back to camp, leading the mule behind. Reuben started on the back trail, standing in his stirrups and shading his eyes as he looked toward the road but saw nothing close. The tracks of the mule sided the willows and the river, but within about a mile, Reuben saw the tracks came from the roadway. He turned Blue that direction but was stopped by movement in the willows. He slipped the Henry from the scabbard and started back toward the riverbank only to find three more mules, grazing contentedly as they stepped over their traces to maneuver for more grass. A quick glance showed two more mules across the river, also grazing but had lifted their heads at the sight of the man on the horse.

Reuben shook his head and backed Blue from the willows and began searching for the trail of the mules and soon found where they had come from the roadway. He glanced to his left and saw Levi approaching on the yellow horse, waved him close and when he neared, "I found the other mules. They're back there by the water, grazing. Two are across the river, but I don't think they're going anywhere. Let's go to the road," he pointed with the muzzle of his Henry to the tracks leading into the willows, "I'm thinkin' there's a wagon or somethin' in the ditch, yonder," nodding to the road.

Levi followed Reuben's lead, slipped the Henry from the scabbard beneath the right fender leather of the saddle and brought the rifle across the pommel. He followed Reuben, looking all about for any sign of life. As they neared the two-track roadway, they noticed the tracks of the mules and looked down the road to the east. About sixty yards away, just off the road, on its side, lay a stagecoach. Reuben reined up, looking all about, searching the flats and rolling hills for any sign of life, but seeing none, nudged Blue onwards.

They walked slowly, eyes constantly roving about, watching for any movement and listening for anything that would be a giveaway, but all was silent and still. Nearing the stage, Reuben reined up Blue, stood in his stirrups to search the brush that surrounded the stage. He noted the door had been flung open and lay askew. He called out, "Hello! Anybody around?" He waited, holding his rifle across his chest, thumb on the hammer to bring it to full cock if necessary.

"Hello!" came a weak voice, but not from the stage. Beyond the brush, a cluster of juniper and piñon shielded the source. "Are you friendly?"

"Yes! We're here to help, we found the mules and backtracked them," explained Reuben, watching the trees.

"Help me, then! Don't just sit there, you can't do a body any good just gawkin'!" came the voice, a little stronger but still a little strange. Reuben thought it might be a woman, but maybe some milquetoast city slicker. He stepped down, still holding his rife at the ready and started toward the trees. He motioned for Levi to stay where he was until he got a sign from Reuben.

He stepped to the edge of the trees, saw a gingham skirt wrapped around a sizable woman who knelt beside an injured man. She turned to look at Reuben and said, "Well? You gonna help or not?" and motioned Reuben to her side in a way that made Reuben instantly respond. He chuckled to himself and answered, "Yes ma'am!" as he knelt beside the man opposite the woman.

"I'm Maude. Maude Riley. We was on our way to the gold diggin's when a bunch o' rebels took chase and ran the stage off'n the road. They kilt the shotgunner and two passengers but didn't dare lay a hand on me! The driver here's hurt a mite, took a shot in his back. I got the bullet out, patched him up some, but he needs more help'n I can give." She struggled to her feet and put hands on her hips, looking down at both the unconscious driver and Reuben. "Think you can do any better?"

"Uh, no ma'am. But we got a couple women back at camp that might be able to, they've got bandages and such. "Uh, I'm Reuben, Reuben Grundy, and that fella yonder is Levi Green." As they spoke, Reuben stood and motioned to Levi to come near, he glanced to the wounded man, then asked Levi, "You think you could get that door free," pointing to the stagecoach door. "If you can, maybe we can use it to carry this man."

"I can sure give it a try!" declared Levi.

Maude looked from one man to the other, glanced down at the wounded driver just as the man stirred, moaned and let a raspy breath escape, and lay still. Maude shook her head, looked to Reuben, "Won't be needin' the door," as she nodded toward the driver.

Maude was every bit as tall as Reuben, not quite as broad shouldered, but definitely broader in the beam. She was a woman used to making her own way and taking no gruff from anyone. Reuben shook his head as he thought of the rebels' response when they confronted her, they were probably more scared of her than she was of them. When Levi offered her his horse, she stepped close and looked at Levi, "Well, get down there and let me have your knee to get on this animal!" motioning to Levi to kneel down so his knee would be a step stool for her.

"Yes'm," replied a wide-eyed Levi as he dropped his eyes, appearing afraid to look directly at the big woman. When he knelt, she nodded, hiked up her skirt and stepped on his knee and swung her leg over the horse's rump to seat herself behind the saddle. She looked at Levi, "Well, ain'tchu gonna get on?" motioning to the open saddle.

"Yes'm," replied Levi, again dropping his eyes as he hopped up to put one foot in the stirrup, but unable to swing his leg over the back of the horse, he struggled to slip his leg over the seat of the saddle and drop into place. Maude had grabbed up the tie downs behind the cantle and said, "Alright then, let's get a move on!"

———

THE WOMEN TRIED TO MAKE OVER MAUDE, BUT SHE shushed them and waved them off, "Just give me somethin' to eat an' I'll be alright," she insisted. As they ate, she explained to the others what had happened with the stage. "They came up behind us, started shootin' right off. The two fellas in the stage with me tried shootin' out the windows but they couldn't hit nothin'. The shotgunner wounded one of 'em, but he took a bullet an' fell off. Then when we tipped over, they stopped. Then they demanded the strongbox under the boot, but the driver wouldn't give it, so they shot him. When the other'ns inside were made to get out, they shot 'em down soons they hit the ground. When I tried climbin' out, one o' em wanted to shoot me too, but their leader said, 'We don't shoot wimmen!' kinda whined it, ya' know?" She shook her head at the memory, dabbed a tear, "And when I got clear and stood lookin' at 'em I asked, 'Your mommas know what you're up to?'" She chuckled, shaking her head again, "I don't think they liked that, but they took the strongbox an' left. That's when I dragged the driver into the trees, case they come back. The other'ns are in the brush behind the stage." She breathed heavy, looked at Elly and dropped her gaze as she remembered.

Reuben let the silence lay for a moment, then looking at Levi, "We've got us some buryin' to do. You had enough to eat?"

"Yassuh. I'm ready." He rose and looked at Reuben, "We gonna try to get that stage up?"

"Maybe. At least we need to round up the mules."

"I can get the harness patched enough so we can use the mules to pull the stage upright, if'n you want to."

"We'll give it a try," answered Reuben. He looked at the women, "We might as well make this our camp for the night. It'll take us a while to get all that done, but if we get back in time, we might try to get us a deer for some meat."

"You go on and tend to them animals and the buryin', us women can take care of the rest," ordered Maude, already taking charge.

Reuben glanced to a shrugging and smiling Elly, grinned and turned to the horses. With a wave to Levi, the men started from the camp and the women started their chores.

6 / DRIVING

"I'll drive it!" declared Maude as she stood, hands on hips, glowering at the two men that stood beside the now upright stagecoach. The women had saddled up and joined the men, more out of curiosity than a need to help, but the men had already used the gathered mules with patched harnesses to pull the coach upright and back on the roadway.

Reuben frowned, "You? Levi here's gonna drive it! 'Sides, we still have harness and such to take care of before anybody drives anything. But what makes you think you can drive a stagecoach?"

"Cuz I used to drive my father's freight wagons, and did it better'n any man!" retorted Maude, shaking her finger at Reuben and Levi.

The men looked at one another and Levi whispered, "I ain't gonna argue with her, you?"

"Uhuhh, nope!" replied Reuben turning back to the stage to check the running gear.

"It's going to be getting dark soon, you want me'n Estrella to go see if we can get some fresh meat?" asked

Elly, smiling at her man, knowing he was not about to broach an argument with Maude.

Reuben grinned at his woman, knowing she was every bit as good a hunter as he was and knew she would probably get a deer for their meat, and it would be a good time for her to share with Estrella. He nodded, "You go on and do that, but take Bear with you just in case you need protection." He motioned to the big dog to go with Elly and Bear rose and trotted to her side without so much as a glance back to Reuben. Reuben shook his head, knowing Bear preferred the company of the women anyway, not that he could blame him.

"Then while you an' the girl there are off galavantin', me'n Precious will get started on supper," declared Maude.

"Uh, Maude, didn't you say this was the maiden run of the stage, I think you said it was a Barlow and Sanderson stage, is that right?" asked Reuben, nodding to the name on the door that had been muddied and scraped beyond legibility.

"That's what I said. That's the only reason I could afford to take the stage, they was offerin' cheap tickets for the maiden run from Colorado City to Fairplay, an' my man ain't done all that well with his gold claim yet," explained Maude, turning away and stepping aboard the pack mule.

As they watched the women leave, Reuben turned to Levi, "The way I heard it in Cañon City, there were several companies competing for stage runs to haul gold and mail from the diggings. As to the Barlow and Sanderson, all I heard about them was usually the company followed the Cherokee Trail from Bent's Fort and Pueblo to Denver, but they were looking to expand and had their sights on the southern portion of the state to include the gold fields of South Park, and also expected to expand using the Santa Fe trail into the San Luis Valley and south." He shook his head as he looked at the stage, checking the thoroughbraces and undercarriage. "Far as I can tell, it looks alright, but I s'pose you know more about them than I do. Whaddya think, Levi?"

"When you was finishin' them graves, I looked over the stage while it was on its side an' I din't see anything damaged too bad. I reckon the worst was on that side that it landed on, the door an' such, but even that wasn't too bad, what with the deep grass an' such."

"You look over the rest of the harness, double tree, an' the rest of it?" asked Reuben.

"Ummhmm, shore did. I reckon I got it put together alright, leastways till we get to town an' have the tools an' such to fix it all proper."

"Then let's get this back to our camp, unhitch the mules and let 'em get some graze an' such. It'll be a long day tomorrow. And ..." he grinned as he remembered something from his last trip through this part of the country, "I think I know something the women will enjoy, us too." He chuckled as he thought of the surprise it would be for the women, especially.

When they pulled up at the camp, Reuben spoke softly to Levi, "If you'll unhitch and tether the mules, I'll get some other things ready, and we'll all take a short ride."

Levi recognized the conspiratorial expression on the grinning face of Reuben, and he smiled, nodded and said, "Right away."

Reuben saw Elly getting her appaloosa ready for their hunt and he walked to her side, "Uh, I think I'll do the hunting, but first, I think you ladies need to come with us."

Elly frowned, cocked her head to the side, "What are you up to now?" she asked, grinning at her man and seeing the grin tugging at the corners of his mouth.

"You'll see. I'll get some things together and be right with you. Make sure everybody's got a ride, we'll be goin' a couple miles or so."

The entourage was soon on their way, Reuben and Bear leading with Elly by his side. Maude had commandeered Levi's mule and everyone else rode a horse with Levi leading their mule loaded with the goods gathered by Reuben and stuffed into the panniers without anyone knowing what he was doing.

It was a short ride and as they neared, a steam cloud rose lazily up from beyond the trees and Elly was the first to spot it, causing her to frown as she looked at Reuben, "Is that ...?"

Reuben chuckled, nodding, "Ummhumm, shore is!" he declared as he motioned for the others to follow him to the trees. The steam cloud rose from a wide pool, bubbling water flowing into it from a small stream coming from the gurgling hot springs. Elly looked at Reuben and back to the pool, "Can we?"

"Be careful, it'll probably be pretty hot near the spring, but you can. Levi and I will be on the other side of the chokecherries yonder, and you'll have all the privacy you want. But I might go for some meat while you're bathing and maybe washing some clothes, if you want, but Levi will stand guard. I won't be long, then it'll be our turn."

The women were giddy at the opportunity to bathe, especially in hot water, which was a definite luxury in the mountains. Elly had previously prepared some soap from yucca roots and the ladies used it for both bathing and on the clothes. The women savored their time and were reluctant to get out, but the sun was lowering, and they wanted the men to have their turn, so once clothed, they called for Levi and saw Reuben returning with the carcass of a deer over the pack saddle of the mule and motioned him to the pool.

As they started back to camp, dusk was dimming the light and Elly smiled at her man, "Thank you for that! It was wonderful! And I know everyone enjoyed it, but now, it's getting dark, we need to butcher the deer and get some supper going, so, you're going to have to help!"

"Don't I always?" asked Reuben, looking seriously at Elly.

"Ha! Only when you can't find an excuse to get out of it!" chuckled Elly. Estrella was behind them and heard the conversation and added, "She's right, you know. I don't recall you ever doing the cooking."

Elly grinned at Reuben, "By the way, what's the plan regarding the stage hold-up? We goin' after that band of Rebels?"

Reuben shook his head, "Not right away. Too many of 'em for just the two of us, but I reckon we'll be hearing more about them soon. Didn't really want to give away our standing, you know, bein' marshals and such. Figure we might find out more just listening, you know how folks love to talk."

"Did they get much from the stage?"

"Not according to Maude. She said this was the first run into the park for that company and I don't reckon they were carrying much, but she didn't know for sure. She said they got the strongbox and took everything from the passengers before they killed 'em, so, hard telling how much they got until we talk to someone from the stage line."

"Will we make Fairplay tomorrow?"

"Should, maybe late afternoon. Then we can settle in there, get us some rooms at the hotel. Levi wants to find the smithy and see if he can get work. I don't know if the town has a sheriff or marshal, but if so, I'll need to talk to him."

The refreshed group split the chores and soon had a good meal sizzling over the cookfire and fresh coffee dancing on the rock. They soon turned in for the night, taking to their blankets protected by the cluster of juniper and piñon and with deep grass for their comfort, leaving guard duty to Bear and the animals, knowing they would detect anything long before anyone else.

Elly and Reuben lay together, hands behind their heads as they looked at the stars in the black velvet night sky. "The stars are so beautiful, don't you think?" asked Elly.

"I do! And it seems out here in the west, they're so close we can almost reach up and touch them!" answered Reuben, whispering softly to his bride.

She reached over and tucked her hand under his arm, rolling to her side to face him, "But everything is more beautiful here in the mountains, especially when I'm with you!"

"Why, Mrs. Grundy, you took the words right out of my mouth!" declared Reuben, turning to face Elly and pull her close for a good night kiss.

7 / REBELS

"There was nothin' but greenbacks in that strongbox!" declared Jim Reynolds, venting his rage against his brother, John.

"What's wrong with greenbacks? We can use 'em to get supplies, anywhere we want!" replied the younger Reynolds, glowering back at his brother.

"The plan was to get into the park without anyone knowing, then hit selected stages and more to get the bigger hauls, meaning gold!"

"We need to eat in the meantime or were you planning on storming the town and robbing the emporium of all the beans and pickles?" grumbled John.

"Alright, but from now on, don't get so impatient and go out on your own again! We want to hit the right stages and more, then, if you remember, the plan was to push to Denver and meet up with Brown's bunch!"

"If you ask me, Brown won't last long enough to even get to Denver. He's no better'n an ol' lady when it comes to leadin' a band of men, especially when they're guerrillas gettin' gold for the confederacy. He can't make a decision till its too late! He won't even get out of his blankets on his own, he has to wait till the sun's in his eyes or somebody rolls him out!" grumbled John. He shook his head as he remembered when the two bands of guerrillas split after coming from Texas and New Mexico to cross into Colorado Territory. While the Reynolds band was to move to South Park and the Brown band to the southeastern flats south of Fort Lyon then to El Pueblo and north to Denver. Their orders were to recruit secessionists, build up their numbers, and move against Denver to turn Colorado into a Southern state for the Confederacy.

John looked to his brother, the leader of their small band of about a dozen, "Look, I know General Cooper said we were to *disrupt supply lines, confiscate gold and ship it south, and gain recruits,* but from what we know of the way the war's goin', I don't see much purpose in doin' all that, even if we thought we could be successful."

Jim looked around their camp, saw the other men gathered in groups, drinking their coffee and finishing the last of the canned peaches, the delicacy picked up when they stopped in Cañon City, and talking among themselves. He nodded to John, motioning him beyond the picket line of horses. As they stood beyond the sight and hearing of the others, Jim lowered his voice and said, "Look, I agree with you. We've talked before about returning to this country and taking our share of the gold in the goldfields, and neither one of us liked the idea of working over a sluice box. Now here's what I'm thinkin', we do just as the general said, but instead of recruiting and disrupting, we focus our efforts on taking gold shipments and money from the stages, freighters, even some of these wealthy ranchers." He grinned when he paused, stepping back and looking around to ensure no one was near and watching the expression on his brother's face.

John was quick to let a broad smile paint his face as he reached out to slap his brother on his shoulder. "Now you're talkin'!"

Jim frowned, "Quiet! I don't want them knowin' what's happenin' 'till we make our first strike! Then when we've got gold in our hands, I don't think any of 'em will argue."

John grinned, "In the meantime, those greenbacks will buy us plenty of supplies! There had to be a couple thousand dollars in that box, an' we can get food and ammo and anything else, you know, like goin' to Buckskin to the tavern where all them wimmen are!" He shook his head, grinning and showing his tobacco-stained teeth. "Ol' Harvey's gonna like this way o' doin' things, you can bet on that!"

"Look, just cuz Harvey Briggs is our brother-in-law don't mean he gets cut in on everything. After all, we're supposed to take care of him for our sis, remember?"

"Yeah, I remember. So, what's next?"

"We'll head north, stay away from the town, maybe send you and Harvey and maybe Addison Stowe into town for supplies. Then we'll meet up at Adolfe Guiraud's ranch; he's got plenty of room for us and the horses. Then we'll plan our next move, probably against the stage line."

"Good, good. Yeah, we can do that. But I reckon we could get us a couple pack mules for the supplies, it's been hard trying to pack enough stuff behind our saddles and such."

"Yeah, with the greenbacks, you can probably pick up a mule at the livery in Fairplay 'fore you get the supplies." He paused, looking around, then with a lop-sided smile, he motioned his brother to follow as they returned to the camp. As they approached, several of the men stood, looking and waiting, knowing they were getting close to what they thought would be action and they were all anxious to know what was next.

Jim Reynolds stood before the men, his brother John slightly to the side, and lifted his hands for the men to be silent and come a little closer. "Men, we've come a long way together. Since signin' up with General Douglas Hancock Cooper and the Third Texas Regiment, we've been to Indian Territory, fought against the Union and the Indians, until General Cooper thought we, most of us having been to Colorado territory before, could be used to raid the military roads and their supplies, recruit locals for the south, and capture gold shipments for the Confederacy." Most of the men nodded and moved about, agreeing with the directive of their assignment. Reynolds continued, "Now, there's only a handful of us and we can't be expected to get into any major engagements, but ..." he looked around and let a slow grin split his face, "I think we can do a good job of capturing some of that gold that's bein' shipped from the big mines in the mountains!" The men cheered as the shipments were mentioned. "Now, I'm not too concerned about spending our time recruiting, I'm just not too anxious to show our faces among the many miners and such, or even to get into a fight to *disrupt!* It just doesn't seem worthwhile to risk getting shot for no gain!" Again, the men cheered their agreement, "So, what we'll be doing is hitting the stages, stations, maybe some of the mines, ranches and such, all for the purpose of gold!"

Jim smiled as he looked at the men, then lowered his eyes only to lift them with a somber expression and a furrowed brow, "So, from now on, when you get an

41

order, you obey it! No questions asked! It's the only way we can succeed in what we have planned." He looked from man to man, recalling each name to mind, knowing not all would survive, but the gain would be worth the price to be paid.

There was Harvey Briggs, their brother-in-law, unimpressive in his own right, but loyal. Anderson Wilson, Addison Stowe, Owen Singletary, Thomas Holloman, all men that had been with them from the beginning of their enlistment and all proven men, fighters all. Thomas Holloman the biggest of the bunch, easily standing more than six feet and weighing over two hundred pounds, he had been a smithy before the war and could lift an anvil in each hand like most men lifted a coffee cup. John Andrews, John T. Bobbitt, and Thomas Knight were newer additions, but already had shown their loyalty and willingness to stand and fight without a question, even though Bobbitt was a bit on the bloody side, more anxious to kill or maim than waste time talking. Jim let his chest swell as he thought of *his* men, men who would be the tools to make him and his brother rich with gold.

He breathed deep, grinned, "Now, let's saddle up, we'll be traveling through most of the park at night. We're too big a group to go unnoticed in the daytime and I don't want word getting out about our presence. We'll travel quietly, but John, Harvey and Addison, will go into town and get supplies and we'll meet up further north at a ranch that belongs to a friend of ours. There we'll plan our next steps and hopefully, our first shipment of gold!"

As they readied to pull out, Jim spoke to his brother, "You and the others take that road by the Middle Fork of the Platte and go on into Fairplay. I'll take the others and we'll stay east of the big ridge; you know the one they call the Spine of the Park?" He grinned when his brother chuckled at the description of the jagged ridge that rode the middle of the park and from the mountain tops it did resemble the backbone of a beast. "We'll go north until we come to the end of the ridge, then cut west and hit Trout Creek, that'll put us about square in the middle of the ranch. We'll be waitin' for you, so don't waste any time, the men'll be almighty hungry."

"Will do! Be seein' you soon!" declared John, digging his heels into the ribs of his big black horse, lifting a hand to wave to his brother as he and the supply detail set out for Fairplay.

8 / FAIRPLAY

"Heeyaaah mules!" shouted Maude, leaning forward to slap the leads on the backs of the six-up team of mules. Maude sat atop the driver's box, Patience beside her, as she hollered and slapped at the team. The stagecoach rocked back on its thorough-braces, wood and leather creaking and complaining, as the mules leaned into their collars and traces and dug deep to start on the road to Fairplay. Maude's luggage and that of the other passengers, now dead and buried, was fastened tight in the rear boot. The strongbox and a few other parcels had been taken by the rebels. Reuben and the others led out, each one astride of their horse, leading the pack animals, and with the stage bringing up the rear, they made quite a cavalcade in the wilderness of the southern end of South Park.

The roadway clung to the shoulder of the long sparsely timbered ridges that parted the park like a dividing line between the fertile grassland of the South Platte from the seemingly endless prairie that held bunch grass, sage brush, and cacti galore. But the two long ridges were split by the Platte that pushed its way between the two, coming from the high mountains beyond Fairplay and Buckskin, to wend its way to the southeast.

The morning light showed a slow-moving herd of buffalo grazing its way north along the waterway, enjoying the green grass of late spring, early summer. Reuben pointed out the rumbling herd, guessing it to number well over a thousand head and maybe twice that many. "If we weren't anxious to get to Fairplay, I'd be sorely tempted to take one o' them buffler, cuz they sure to make good eatin'!" declared Reuben, nodding toward the brown blanket that covered the valley bottom.

"I ain't never had no buffalo 'fore," replied Levi. "We ain't gots too many of 'em back east, an' I never had no rifle big 'nuff to take one."

"Well, maybe after we get settled, we can take a ride out and get us one. They do make for mighty fine eating!" responded Reuben, smacking his lips at the memory.

The two men rode together as they led the entourage and Levi asked, "What time you think we might make it to Fairplay?"

"Oh," began Reuben, shading his eyes as he looked at the morning sun barely peaking over the eastern horizon, "Maybe mid-afternoon, perhaps a little later." He twisted in his saddle to take in the colors of the early morning, the sun painting the bellies of the low-lying clouds that showed dark on top but the undersides a blazing pink shading to deeper red. He remembered his father often saying, "Red sky at morning, Sailor take warning. Red sky at night, sailor's delight."

He knew the words came from the Scriptures but also knew there was truth in the warning, but he was unconcerned about the weather, at least not as concerned as he was about the band of Confederate guerillas that had already shown themselves to be willing to do anything, including murder, to accomplish their mission, if it was a true military mission.

Late morning saw them crossing the Middle Fork of the Platte. The gravelly bottomed crossing was easily made by all, and Reuben signaled a stop, motioning to the grassy riverbank. He stepped down and led Blue to the water even though he had taken his usual drink as they crossed, but Reuben wanted the big horse fresh and well-fed, allowing him to snatch mouthfuls of grass as Reuben ground tied him at the edge of the grass. The others did the same with their mounts as Reuben pointed to the ridge that sided the road, "I'm goin' up there for a quick look around, don't wanna run up on those rebels, cuz I don't think they'd like the idea of us bringing the coach in and tellin' folks what happened. They probably thought it'd be a couple days 'fore anybody came lookin' or they missed the stage."

"Do you want us to make a fire for some coffee?" asked Elly, always aware of her husband's needs and wants.

"Nah, not necessary. We're makin' good time and we might make Fairplay in a couple, maybe three hours, then we can do it up right in the dining room at the hotel." He smiled at his woman, drew her close for a quick embrace and kiss, then turned and started up the long ridge. It was just a short while and he was back with the others, "Didn't see nothin'! So, let's get a move on, sooner started, sooner there!" he declared as he stepped aboard Blue. He motioned Bear to take the scout and nudged Blue to follow after, leading the way for the others.

Mid-afternoon, the group rode into Fairplay on the

east end of Front Street. The livery, with big doors standing open, showed the smithy banging on the anvil but stopped and looked up at the passersby. When he saw the stagecoach, he dropped his hammer, tossed the hot metal in the water trough and stripped off his apron to follow the newcomers into town. He stepped up on the boardwalk and hollered, "Hey! What happened to the coach?" as he pointed at the scuffed and scraped stagecoach.

Reuben reined up, turned to look back at the smithy, "There was a hold-up. Killed ever'body but the woman there," nodding to Maude as she held the reins of the six-up.

"Woman?!" asked the smithy, incredulous at the thought of a woman stage driver. With one hand on his hip, the other shading his eyes, he looked at Maude then back to Reuben, "She is a woman!"

"Of course, I am! And don't you forget it! Now, where do I take this stage?" bellered Maude, the mules tugging at the ribbons as she looked at the smithy.

"Uh, down yonder, end of Front Street. Stage office is there, big sign!" he answered, looking around and seeing a familiar face, lowered his voice and said, "That's a woman drivin' that coach!"

Maude shook her head and slapped reins to the mules, rocking the coach back, and started for the stage station. Reuben led the way, wanting to talk to the Stagers or the Station keeper about the stage and cargo. As they pulled up in front of the office, three men stood on the board walk, appearing to be waiting. A crowd had gathered along the boardwalk and followed the stage most of the way through town, growing in size as they moved. Reuben reined up in front, leaned on the pommel and looked at the men, "Who's the keeper, or super?"

"That'd be me," declared a man with garters holding up his sleeves, a visor shading his eyes and a half-chewed cigar dangling from his mouth.

"Your coach was held up this side of Ute pass, in the flats. Everybody but Maude," nodding to the woman on the boot, "was killed, most everything was taken."

"Well, uh, guess we better get the sheriff, don'tcha think Jake?" declared the first man, looking at a younger man, obviously a hostler that was starting toward the mules to take charge of the animals and the coach. "Uh, sure, whatever you say Mr. Jenkins."

Jenkins nodded to the third man, motioning for him to go for the sheriff, but Reuben stopped him, "If you're going for the sheriff, tell him to meet us in the dining room of the South Park Hotel, we've been travelin' a spell and we're hungry!"

"Yessir, will do, sir!" declared the third man as he started pushing his way through the crowd.

Maude leaned forward, wrapped the ribbons or reins around the brake handle and looked at the station keeper, "Well, help me down sonny!" she barked, motioning to the cigar chewing manager, who quickly stepped to the edge of the coach and reached his hand up to aid Maude as she stepped down on the wheel, then down to the rim to take his hand and make the long step to the ground. She dusted herself off, adjusted her gingham dress and touched her hair, smiled at the keeper and stepped up on the boardwalk to turn around and look to Reuben. "I'm goin' to the hotel, see you there!" she declared. She looked at the keeper, pointed to the top of the coach, "That brown bag with the brass hinges and handle, that'n's mine. Send it and the other'n like it to the hotel!" she ordered and turned her back before he could protest and started toward the hotel.

After getting their horses stabled and tended to, Reuben, Elly, Estrella and Levi and Patience, walked to the South Park Hotel that sat back off Front Street but had quickly become a landmark for the growing town. Maude had already checked in and the clerk explained, "Mrs. Riley said she would join you folks in the dining room shortly. Now, would you folks like some rooms?" he inquired, but gave a disgusted glance at Levi and Patience and looked back at Reuben.

"Yes, we would. I would like a room for me and my wife, a separate room for the young lady," nodding toward Estrella, "and another room for our friends, the Greens."

The clerk sighed heavily, pursed his lips, and leaned forward to whisper to Reuben, "But, we don't allow coloreds in this hotel!"

Reuben shook his head slightly, looking around in the lobby and through the dining room doors, "But you most certainly do! Look there, there's a white man, a pink lady, a brown man, a red man, a tan lady, oh, everywhere I look, everyone is colored! Not a soul is pale white like paper, so, I don't see any problem. The keys please?" he asked, holding out his hand.

"But sir!" protested the clerk.

Reuben frowned, reached into his jacket pocket, pulled out the Deputy Marshal badge and held it out for the clerk to see. "You were saying?" he asked.

"Oh, uh, nothing sir," he stammered, turned away and back with three keys. "All your rooms are on the ground floor, right through there," he said as he pointed to the doorway to the hall leading to the rooms.

"Thank you, and by the way, you didn't see this,"

responded Reuben, patting his pocket where he replaced the badge, then picking up their bedrolls and saddle bags to lead the way.

"Uh, yessir!" nervously answered the clerk as he watched the others. No one in the lobby or the hallway gave them a second glance. The prejudices of the east and the south were not as common in the mountain country, even though there had been many sympathizers of the Southern cause.

They freshened up, changed out of their dusty clothes and were soon seated in the dining room at a table reserved by Maude who happily motioned them to her side. She had also changed and fixed her hair and showed little resemblance to the stage driver that rode into town aboard the stagecoach pulled by six recalcitrant mules that were well handled by a dominant and determined woman.

Reuben saw the drooping handlebar moustache before he saw the man, the big whiskers appeared to stretch across the doorway, but a second look showed a big man, a leather vest covering a faded linsey Woolsey shirt tucked into canvas britches held up by overworked galluses, bushy eyebrows that shaded black piercing eyes and a whiskery face that did not keep close company with a razor. A floppy felt hat was pushed back to reveal sparse dark hair shot with grey to match the whiskers, stooped shoulders showing a lifetime of hard work, but the hardest appeared to be the sporting of a metal star on his chest. He spotted Reuben and company and motioned to the man beside him to follow as he pushed his way through the mostly empty tables and chairs to make his way to Reuben's side. "You the bunch that brought in the stage?" he growled.

Reuben nodded, stood and stretched out his hand, "I'm Reuben Grundy, this is my wife Elly, our friends, Estrella, Maude, Levi and Patience," nodding or pointing to each one as he called them by name. Reuben motioned to the empty chairs opposite him and said, "Have a seat, Sheriff."

"Uh, yeah, I'm Sheriff Jack Sparks, and this is," turning to face the man beside him, "Fauntleroy McElroy, editor of the *Western Mountaineer*, uh, er, the *Miners Journal*, our newspaper." Reuben shook hands with both men, nodded to the chairs for them to be seated. The smaller man was middle-aged, balding, spectacles resting on his nose, and dressed in a waistcoat, frock jacket, and wool trousers. The newspaper man pulled out a stub of a pencil, wet it on his tongue, and with a pad of paper before him, looked up at Reuben, waiting.

The others had already given their order, but when the waitress saw the two men join them at the table, she returned for their order to which the sheriff replied, "Just coffee for us, Mabel."

The sheriff watched the waitress retreat then turned to Reuben, "So, tell me what happened?"

Reuben chuckled as he dropped his head, glanced at the others and looked at the sheriff, "We were coming from Cañon City, stopped at the South Platte after we came over Currant Creek Pass, and spotted a loose mule. After catching him up, and backtracking him, we found the stage." Reuben continued with the story of the robbed stage and finding Maude, burying the others and making their way to Fairplay.

"So, you think it was the Confederates you was followin'?" asked the sheriff.

"Well, Sheriff, we never saw the men, we can only assume they were Confederates after what we were told in Cañon City, but Maude confirmed what we thought. She didn't think much of them, wasn't too sure they were Confederate guerillas, but she described them like the others in Cañon City."

"They didn't act like soldiers to me!" declared Maude, interjecting herself in the conversation. "I ain't never seen no soldiers just shoot down reg'lar folks and then rob their bodies. They weren't interested in what anyone thought about no slaves or nuthin', they just wanted money!"

The newspaper man asked, "Were you traveling with your slaves ma'am?"

"Mind your tongue you little whippersnapper! These folks are my friends and I ain't never had no slaves and never will and anybody that does ought to be horse-whipped, and I'll be the first to volunteer to peel their hide with a black snake bullwhip!" spouted Maude, prompting everyone to look wide-eyed her way as she settled back into her chair, huffing and puffing.

The sheriff looked from Maude to Reuben and asked, "Do you have anything to add to that report?"

"Just to ask a few questions, sheriff. What kind of trouble have you had with secessionists or rebels or whatever they want to call themselves?"

"Well, there's plenty folks that have sympathies with the South around here, and there have been some scrapes and wrestlin' matches, but nothin' much to speak of, at least not recently. Now a while back there was a bunch that tried recruiting others and formed the *Buck-skin Greys*, but they said it was just for protection from the Indians, and they talked big for a while, but most of 'em settled down to workin' their claims and lookin' for gold.

"There were a couple companies of Unionists that went south to fight at Glorieta Pass, but most o' them come back and returned to mining, although they get together ever onct in a while."

"I was familiar with that," explained Reuben, "We,"

nodding to his wife, "were around here and involved in the chase of the Espinoza brothers and were familiar with those that were sympathizers with the confederacy." He paused, sipped at his coffee, "The reason I'm asking sheriff, is if this bunch keep doin' what they started, the whole of South Park could be in for a pretty rough time."

The sheriff frowned, cocked his head to the side, "What is it to you? You plannin' on settlin' around here, maybe do some prospectin'?"

Reuben nodded to the newspaperman, "Mr. McElroy, could you give us a couple minutes in private, please?"

"Certainly, certainly," responded the smaller man, nodding and rising to leave. He looked down at the seated sheriff, "I'll stop by your office later, Jack."

The sheriff nodded, waited for the man to leave and looked at Reuben, "As I said, just what are your plans?"

Reuben slowly shook his head, reached into his pocket and produced his badge so only the sheriff could see, "This is between you and me. We," nodding toward Elly, "are both deputies and we've been sent by the governor to see what we can do about this problem. The governor thinks this could get out of hand."

"So, this is all to be secret?" asked the sheriff, frowning in confusion.

"For the time being at least. Anonymity might give us the opportunity to pick up some information that wouldn't necessarily come our way otherwise."

"And you'll keep me informed as to anything that you find?" asked the sheriff.

"How far does your authority go, sheriff?"

"Well, for now, just here in town. But they're talkin' about Colorado becomin' a state and makin' counties and such, so ..." he explained, shrugging. He frowned,

"Wait, did I hear you say you *and* your wife are deputies?"

Reuben grinned, nodding, "Ummhmm."

"I ain't never heard o' such a thing, a woman deputy?" he scowled, glancing to the petite and pretty Elly, who sat close enough to Reuben to have heard everything that had been said.

Elly smiled, "There's a first time for everything, Sheriff. But don't let it bother you, I've already been well proven with Rebels, highwaymen, Indians, and more and here I sit, and they're pushin' up posies!" Her sweet smile and mischievous glint in her eye made the sheriff frown and twist nervously in his seat before looking back to Reuben.

Reuben smiled, "We will keep you informed of anything that is of concern, and we trust you will do the same?"

"Of course. And I'll take care of the stage company and any goods they need to send to the families of the dead ones." He shook his head, "The driver was a friend of mine, shore hate to hear that happened," he mumbled as he rose from his chair. With a glance back to Reuben and Elly, the Sheriff left the room, leaving the others to enjoy their meal that was just delivered to the table. Reuben turned back to the others and looking at the steak, potatoes, gravy, biscuits and asparagus, he smiled and lifted his fork and knife, only to be stopped by Elly with her hand on his arm, "Will you ask the Lord's blessing?"

"Oh, uh, yes, of course," he replied, a little embarrassed, but bowed his head and began his prayer of thanksgiving. His amen was echoed by the others and they enjoyed their first store bought meal in a long time.

"So, Maude, you think you'll be able to find your husband all right?" asked Reuben, reaching for a biscuit.

"Oh, I already know where to find him. I'll be hiring a wagon and getting to his diggings first thing in the morning. He's got a cabin waitin' and I'm anxious to find him!" she declared smiling and showing a little more vulnerability than she had before.

"How can we help you and Patience, Levi?

"I'm thinkin' 'bout tryin' to talk to the smithy at the livery. With this town as busy as it is, he might use some help. And if not, then we'll take ol' Mabel, the mule, and make our way up the valley. They says there's a couple other towns thataway and I might get some work there."

"Well, we're not sure exactly when or if we'll be leaving, but in the meantime, if we can be of help, you be sure to let me know, will you?"

"Yessuh, you've already been a big help an' we 'preciate that ver' much!" he declared, using his biscuit to push the last bit of meat onto his fork, anxious to enjoy every bite.

It was early the next morning when the small party went their separate ways, Maude driving the wagon with her meager belongings as she headed for the diggings beyond Buckskin, and Levi walking to the livery to talk to the smithy. When Reuben saw Levi returning with a broad smile he asked, "Good luck?"

"Yassuh, the smithy he be mighty glad to get some help an' he says we can stay in the tack rook till we gets a cabin. When I tol' him my woman's a good cook, he grinned ear to ear and said he'd be happy to pay her to cook for him too!"

"Well Levi, I'm happy to hear that. I'm sure you'll do fine." He turned to look at Elly who stood by his side,

"When we come back through here, we'll be sure to stop in and see how you're doing."

"We be lookin' for'd to that Reuben, Elly. Thank you again!" he declared. "I gots to go tell Patience!"

"So, what's next, Cap'n?" asked one of the younger men, Owen Singletary.

"Captain? I'm not a captain! My name is Jim, that's what I answer to, so use my name. 'Sides, we don't want anybody hearing you use rank and such, that'll be a dead giveaway that we're soldiers, or supposed to be, anyway,"

"Whaddya mean, supposed to be, ain't we so'jers?" asked the big man, John Bobbitt.

"Well, yes and no," replied Jim Reynolds, looking around at the men gathered in the barn of his friend, Adolphe Guiraud. He looked out the open door, and back to the men. "I need to tell you somethin' men. When John and the others went into Fairplay for supplies, John picked up a recent copy of the Rocky Mountain News," he held up the paper for the men to see, "and there's somethin' mighty interestin' in it. Now, we'd heard about a big battle at Gettysburg, but didn't know much about it. It seems that was the biggest battle of the war, and the Union done stomped all over our boys in grey, killed more in that one battle than most of the rest of the war! While our boys killed o'er five thousand of the Union, we lost more'n five times that number, over twenty-eight thousand. Now, most are thinkin' that battle marks the beginning of the end. The latest news," he pointed at the article titled *News from the Front* "says Grant Given Command, Union Forces pushing South." He paused, looking around to let the news be devoured. He knew the men were no different than him and his brother, believing every one of them had at one time or another considered deserting and returning home or going somewhere to make their own way away from the war, discouragement was one thing they all had in common. He glanced from one man to the other, seeing the hopelessness in their eyes, then continued. "Now, the way things are bein' told and the way I see it, any gold or such that we get here in the mountains ain't gonna make a lick o' difference to the outcome of the war! So, here's what I figger on doin'. We will continue to have our way about things, cuz there's plenty o' gold bein' shipped outta here on the stages, and there's folks that got some stashed away, gold, greenbacks, and such. Now, I think this is the only chance we're gonna get to get us our share of things and get set-up for whatever we choose to do after this war is over. So, instead of shippin' gold to the confederacy, we'll just divide it among ourselves, maybe stash some of it away and keep on doin' what we know how to do as long as it pays. When we all get us a goodly sum, then we'll just go our separate ways and make a life doin' what we want, wherever we want!"

The men were a little surprised at what their leader was saying, but the more they heard, the better it sounded, especially the part about sharing the gold. Broad smiles split faces and the men started talkin' with one another, slapping hands and shouting, hopelessness had turned to excitement, and several with the first tidbit of hope and a reason to look forward to tomorrow, started dancing some kind of jig. The Reynolds brothers laughed with the others, shaking their head and looked at one another, John slapped his brother on the shoulder, "Looks like we're in business brother!"

"Indeed, it does! Now, I've got to go talk to Adolphe, I want to find out about the stage that comes outta Buckskin. If it's like it was, there's usually a pretty good amount of gold that gets shipped from there and I'm thinkin' that would be a good start for our new venture!" He looked at the men, their excitement and anticipation of riches kept them jabbering and jostling one another, and he turned back to John, "Try to keep them in line, I don't want to have to explain to Adolphe what they're all excited about." As he took a last glance to the men, Jim Reynolds turned away and started for the house.

He knocked on the back door of the farmhouse, glimpsed Mrs. Guiraud carrying the water bucket to the well, but hearing the voice of his friend, Adolphe, to enter, Jim Reynolds walked through the door and greeted his friend. "Good mornin' Adolphe, is that coffee I smell?"

"It is, would you care for some?" answered the big German.

"Of course, I can't turn down good coffee?" replied Jim, taking the chair by the table as directed by Adolphe.

"So, what are your plans?" asked Guiraud as he seated himself at the table, the steaming cups of coffee sitting before them.

"I've got a letter I need to get out and I was rememberin' there was a stage that comes from Buckskin and goes to Denver. Is that still runnin'?" he asked.

"Ja, Ja." He glanced at the big pendulum clock ticking

on the wall and said, "It usually leaves Buckskin at first light, stops all along the way and well, usually passes on the road yonder 'bout noon or so. Then it stops at the Scotsman's ranch, McLaughlin's, it's a stage station."

Jim looked at the clock, saw it was about half past nine, and nodded. "Good, good. That gives me time to finish it up and make it to the station." He took a big sip of coffee, "We'll be leavin' this mornin', headin' for Denver City but not in any big hurry."

"Got business there?" asked Adolphe.

"Yeah, well, not so much business. We've got an uncle in business there and he needs some help finishin' up his building since that fire 'most wiped him out. So, this bunch with me would make a good crew and we could get him up and goin' in short order." He took another big gulp of coffee, sat the cup down and stood, extending his hand to his friend. "We are mighty grateful for the use of your barn, you're a good friend, Adolphe."

"Anytime. That's what friends are for, right?" responded a smiling Guiraud. Standing, he was almost a head taller than Jim, and about fifty pounds heavier. His big ham hock sized mitt swallowed Jim's smaller hand and the big German shook it heartily. Jim grinned up at the man, and as he released his hand, "Thanks again! Maybe we'll see you next time we come through!"

"Ja, Ja," replied the grinning rancher.

When Jim walked into the barn, he ordered the others, "Let's load up! We're leavin' right away, need to make it to Hamilton within the hour!"

"How far's Hamilton, Cap'n," asked Singletary, grinning at his use of Captain.

"It's 'bout an hour. It's a stage stop, and we need to get there before the stage."

Singletary slowly nodded, understanding the need to

beat the stage, assuming the stage would be taken by the men and hopefully begin their haul of gold. He turned quickly, clapped hands and hollered at the others, "C'mon fellas! We gotta get a move on!" and ran to the stall with his horse and began saddling the dapple grey. Others were hustling about, saddling horses and under the direction of John Reynolds, four men were busy with the pack saddles and panniers for the pack mules they bought in Fairplay. The word seemed to spread among the men that they were getting ready to strike a stage and there was gold to be had and the mood lifted, and each man was already formulating his own plans for his share of the riches.

As Jim finished saddling his horse, he glanced around the barn at the men, all busy with their animals and gear, but one man, the big John Bobbitt came through the back door, fussing with the buttons on his britches and looking a little sheepish. Jim thought it was nothing more than the man probably had to relieve himself and was hurrying to get to his horse. But something was off, even though Jim couldn't set his mind on it, choosing to tuck it away in his mind to mull over later. He shook his head, led his black gelding out of the stall and looked at the men, "Alright, let's mount up and put some dust behind us!" He swung aboard and dropped into the seat of his saddle, dug heels into the gelding's ribs and started from the barn at a trot, motioning to the men that followed to get a move on and took to the roadway away from the ranch house.

Hamilton was on the north bank of Tarryall Creek and was the first settlement in South Park, but when the competing town of Tarryall City was started just across the creek, things began to decline, even though the gold diggings prospered. Because of the rivalry, Dan

McLaughlin landed the contract to have a stage station at his ranch, just south a few miles from the competing towns. Jim looked at his brother, "John, as I remember it, McLaughlin's is far enough from Hamilton that whatever happens there won't be known in town, am I right?"

"The way I remember it, the ranch is at least a couple miles from town, so, yeah, nobody in town will know. What'chu thinkin'?"

"The road past the station leads to Breckenridge and over the mountains to California Gulch. Now the way I remember it, they ship gold from both those places, and it goes on the stage that stops at Hamilton!" he grinned as he glanced to his brother.

"You're right! And the Orphan Boy mine is over there, and it's supposed to be a mighty rich mine!" He chuckled, "We just might hit it big, brother!" declared an enthusiastic John, looking to his older brother, who just grinned and nodded.

A long timbered ridge pushed into the park, a knobby hill at the end. Jim pointed it out to his brother, "Look, McLaughlin's Ranch is just east of that knob, and that's a stop for the Hinkley and Company stage that comes out of Buckskin. But further up there by Tarryall Creek, at Hamilton, there's another stage stop for Kehler and Montgomery Stage Line. I'm thinkin' the Montgomery stop will have the gold from the Tarryall Diggings and McLaughlin's and Hinkley company is the stop for the stage from Buckskin and Fairplay and maybe Breckenridge and California Gulch. So, if we split up, one bunch'll hit McLaughlin's and the other will take the Witter station in Hamilton. We can join up downstream of Tarryall Creek and go on from there."

"Yeah, good idea, cuz I was thinkin' if we approach a station with this many," nodding to the nine men following, "it'd scare folks, make 'em think somethin' was happening and put 'em on guard. But with just five or six of us, folks wouldn't be too concerned."

"Now you're thinkin'," answered Jim. He had reined up and stopped the company, turned to John and back to the men, "We're gonna split up and hit two stations." He motioned to his brother-in-law, Harvey Briggs, to come alongside. "Anderson, you and Addison, Jackson, Owen, you men come with me. The rest of you will go with John. Now, all we're doing is hitting some stage stations, and any stages that may come in while we're there. No reason for a bunch of shootin' an' killin' folks, that just makes the rest of the country mad, and they come after us, but if it's just money that's gone, they're not as mad and not as brave. So, keep that in mind and do as you're told!" He looked from one to the other, getting a nod of agreement from each one. He turned to his brother, nodded, and led his band away as John took the others further north on the roadway.

11 / STATIONS

The log building used as a stage station on McLaughlin's ranch was also the main ranch house. The main room had been converted to the stage office and held the counter and storage space for shipments. As Jim Reynolds and his company rode into sight, Dan McLaughlin stepped from the house and greeted the riders, "Howdy men, somethin' I can do for ye?" he asked, looking at the small group, his suspicions raised. He dropped his hand to the pistol in his belt and looked from man to man until the man that appeared to be their leader answered.

"Yessir, I've got some letters here that need to be mailed and I heard this was a stage stop. Any chance o' getting' my mail on the stage?" asked Jim Reynolds, leaning on his pommel as he looked at the station keeper, smiling and doing his best to look nonthreatening.

"Sure, sure," answered McLaughlin, relaxing and motioning to Jim to come inside. He watched the other men as Harvey Briggs asked, "Can we water our horses?" nodding to the water trough beside the cabin.

"Go right ahead fellas," answered McLaughlin, turning to lead the leader of the group into the station. As he turned, Jim stepped close behind him, pulled his Colt Navy pistol from his belted holster and held it at his side as he walked into the room. Harvey Briggs followed Jim and the other men stood guard outside, with Addison Stowe standing near the open door. As McLaughlin stepped behind the counter and turned to Jim, he was surprised when Jim lifted the pistol, "Where's your strongbox?" he demanded.

"Now see here, you can't be doin' this! Who do you think you are?" pleaded the station keeper.

"I'm Jim Reynolds and these are just a few of my men, and if you want to live, get with it! Where's the strongbox?" he barked.

Unnoticed by Reynolds, a man stood from the shadows and shook a cane at him, "Here, here! Stop that this instant!" demanded the man who appeared to be in his upper forties or early fifties. Mutton chop whiskers bounced as he spoke, but steely eyes showed the man was used to having authority and the remnants of a uniform jacket told he had been an officer.

"Who are you?" asked Reynolds, motioning to Harvey to cover the man.

"I'm Major H. H. DeMary and I will not stand for this outrage!" demanded the older man.

"And just what do you think you can do about it?" asked Harvey Briggs, waving his pistol before the man.

"Uh, uh, you young whippersnapper, I'm not afraid of you! I'll have you know I was in the Army at the battle of Mexico City, and I also fought for the Union at the Battle of Bull Run!"

Harvey grinned, looked at Jim, "Can you give me any

reason why I shouldn't shoot this windbag? He's already given me enough of an excuse just to shoot him down!"

The former officer stuttered and stammered and waved his cane at Harvey until Harvey stepped forward, lifted his pistol high and brought it down on the side of the head of the blustery man, knocking him to the floor, unconscious. He turned to face McLaughlin, "You ain't got that strongbox yet?" cocking the hammer on his Colt with a loud click.

"I'm gettin' it!" stated McLaughlin, shaking his head and mumbling something about crooks and thieves.

When the station keeper dragged the strongbox from behind the counter, Reynolds looked at the box, back at the keeper and said, "Well, open it!" waving the pistol before him.

The keeper dug the key from his britches pocket, dropped to one knee beside the box, and opened the lock and lid to reveal four bags of gold dust, each bag marked, *Orphan Boy Mine*. Reynolds grinned, looked to Harvey who was also grinning, and summoned Addison. The two men grabbed two bags each, leaving a stack of currency and a bag of gold coin for Reynolds, but he called for help, "Wilson, get in here." He pointed to the rest of the cash and coin, "Before you take that, tie up the keeper there and stuff a rag in his mouth."

As Reynolds and Wilson started from the station, they heard the approach of the stage. Jim called to the others, "Get the horses to the barn and duck out of sight!" then turned to Wilson, "Take the rest of this and put it with the other and tell Harvey to get back here and come with him but stay behind the station."

As the coach came to a stop in front of the station, the shotgunner stepped down and waited for the driver to follow. As they started for the station, the driver said,

"Where's McLaughlin, he usually meets us, and the hostler comes from the barn." He reached out to touch the shotgunner to stop him just as Reynolds stepped from the station.

"Howdy fellas," greeted Reynolds, grinning as he lifted his Colt toward the two.

"Hey, what is this?" demanded the shotgunner, starting to reach for his sidearm but stopped when Reynolds shook his head, grinning and pointing the Colt at the man's belt buckle.

"This is a hold-up," explained Jim. He motioned to Harvey and Wilson to come around and asked the driver and the shotgunner, McClelland, who also was the owner of the stage, "So, where's the strongbox?"

"Get it yourself," growled the driver. Reynolds sneered at the man, lifted his Colt and dropped the hammer. The big pistol roared, bucked, and spat lead that drove into the driver's belly, cut his backbone, and erupted in a splatter of blood out his back. The driver crumpled to the side and Reynolds calmly turned to the other man, "Strongbox?"

"In the driver's boot!" answered the McClelland, shaking his finger in the direction of the stage, his face white and looking like he was about to lose his breakfast.

Reynolds motioned for Harvey to get the strongbox and turned to McClelland, "Now, you give me your money and that nice looking watch in your pocket there," motioning with the pistol to the pocket in the man's vest that did little to hide the gold watch. Harvey struggled with the strongbox but finally dropped it to the ground and jumped down beside it. Reynolds looked around, saw a pickaxe leaning against the side of the station and motioned to Harvey to get it and use it to open the strongbox. Once the box was open, it revealed another six bags of gold, prompting Reynolds and Harvey to both start laughing.

"Come here and tie this'n up with the station keeper. Maybe it'll give us a little time to get away from here and back to Fairplay!" Harvey looked askance at Jim, nodded and directed McClelland into the station.

THE CLAPBOARD BUILDING HAD BEEN WHITEWASHED, BUT now showed little sign of white, save beside the doorway and windows. John Reynolds and his men rode slowly up to the station, looking about for any potential problems, but his attention was caught when a woman stepped from the station, saw the men and continued toward the edge of town, a parasol in hand. John Bobbitt grumbled, "I think I'd like to have *that* instead o' any bag o' gold!"

He was heard by Thomas Holloman who asked, "Are you crazy? If you have a bag of gold, you can buy two or three women just like that!"

"Gold ain't soft and warm like a woman!" mumbled Bobbitt.

John said, "Holloman, you and Andrews are with me. Bobbitt, you, Singletary and Knight stay with the horses, get them out of sight in case a stage comes in, and one is due anytime now, but keep the horses ready."

John Reynolds, Thomas Holloman, and John Andrews walked into the station, pausing to let their eyes adjust to the dim light and looked around. Behind the counter writing something on a pad of paper with a little stub of a pencil, stood Daniel Witter, a stained canvas apron over his linen shirt and wool trousers. He looked up at the three men, "How can I help you gentlemen?" He motioned behind him at the wall of shelves, divided by a doorway into the back room which was their living quarters, "We have a few goods, tobacco, lead, powder, needles, thread, cornmeal, flour, sugar and over there we have barrels with salt pork and pickles." He nodded to his left, "this is the post office, and we can mail just about anything to anywhere."

John stepped forward, leaned an elbow on the counter as he looked at the man, his holstered pistol on the hip away from the counter and he rested his right hand on the butt of the pistol. "So, where do you keep your strongbox?" slipping the Colt Navy revolver from the holster and pointing it at the man's throat.

"Uh, uh, strongbox? What do you mean, strongbox? Only the stages have strongboxes," he stammered, slowly lifting his hands head high and looking from one to the other of the strangers.

"Well, it might not be a strongbox, but what we want is the gold and greenbacks that you have waitin' fer the stage."

"You can't do that! Everything here is United States Mail and it's against the law to take mail!" he stuttered, sweat drops forming on his forehead as his face paled.

John chuckled, glanced to Holloman, "You hear that? It's against the law!" He shook his head and looked back at the station keeper, "Do you really think we care about the law? 'Sides, we're with the Confederacy and we don't recognize your *United States* Law!" spitting the words as his lip curled in a snarl. "Now, do you want us to go searching for that shipment or are you gonna drag it out here, so we don't have to mess up your store and station?"

"Uh, uh, I'll ... I'll get it!" declared Witter as he slowly lowered his hands, stepping back and nodding to the space under the counter. As the keeper bent to get the crate that held four sizeable pouches of gold, the rumble of an approaching stagecoach was heard. John looked at Holloman, "Get out there and get the others hidden until that coach pulls up, then jump 'em!" He looked back at the station keeper as Holloman quickly left the station and could be heard hollering at the others.

John motioned to Andrews to grab the wooden crate and take it out, then looked back at the station keeper, "Now, where's the rest of the money?"

"What money?"

"The money you take in for the store and the money, greenbacks, those lonely prospectors send back to their womenfolk!"

The keeper reached into his pocket and pulled out some folded greenbacks, dug deeper and brought out a handful of coins, most gold. "I don't know what the men send in their letters," he stammered, glancing to a mail pouch that had been readied for the stage. John grabbed up the pouch and spun quickly to smash his pistol on the back of Witter's head, dropping him to the floor.

He stepped to the doorway, bag at his side, lifted it high for the driver of the stagecoach to see, and stepped down as the coach came to a stop. The driver looked down, "Who're you? And where's Dan'l?"

"Dan'l's indisposed for now, but this here's the mail, but you can't have it!" answered a grinning John Reynolds.

"What'chu mean, I can't have it? Hand it over, that's the U.S. Mail!" growled the driver, glancing around, suspicious of the man with the mail bag.

"Well, these other men," nodding to his men that had suddenly appeared from the back of the station, "have first dibs, and they got so many guns, I just didn't want to argue with 'em! And I suggest you don't either!"

declared John, lifting his pistol to threaten the driver and shotgunner. "Now, you just set that shotgun down and climb on down here, real slow like. Oh, and driver, toss that strongbox down before you come down!"

John stepped back as the driver lifted the heavy strongbox and tossed it to the ground just as the shotgunner stepped to the ground beside the stage. There were no passengers, although there were three people walking towards the station, bags in hand, but when they saw the ruckus with men holding guns on the driver and shotgunner, they quickly turned away and hastened back to the town.

The driver stepped down beside the shotgunner, both men standing with hands raised and watching the guerillas ransack the packages in the rear boot. John was guarding the two men, until Bobbitt walked up beside him, his pistol out and pointing at the two men. John glanced at the big man just as Bobbitt pulled the trigger and shot the guard. John looked from Bobbitt to the guard and asked, "What'd you shoot him for?"

"He was goin' for his gun!"

The driver shouted angrily, "The only gun he ever had was his shotgun, and its in the boot!"

Bobbitt growled at him, "Mebbe he shoulda had one! You wanna join him?"

The driver stepped back, eyes wide and arms high as he stuttered, "No, no," but the expression on the big man's face was terrifying and the driver screamed another "NO!" as Bobbitt fired again, dropping the driver in a heap beside the shotgunner.

John Reynolds said, "You fool! Now the whole town's gonna be after us! Get the horses so we can get outta here! NOW!"

"Well, if it isn't the Reverend Dyer! How are you pastor?" declared Reuben, extending his hand to shake with the distinguished character of the mountains. Reverend John L. Dyer, also known as the Snowshoe Itinerant, had spent the last few years ministering to the many prospectors, miners, and others throughout the gold fields. Doubling his time as a mail carrier from California Gulch, Breckenridge, Oro City, and down through Tarryall, Hamilton, Buckskin and Fairplay, he was the most recognized figure in the area.

The Reverend extended his hand, smiling through his long white whiskers, "Reuben, Elly, how good it is to see you two! What brings you back to the high country?"

"Well," Reuben looked around the boardwalk where they stood together, lowered his voice, "the governor asked us to come take a look at the Park and see if we could do something to make sure the gold you carry over the mountain can make it to the Union!"

The Reverend frowned, also glancing around, "Have you heard what happened earlier today?"

Reuben also frowned, "Uh, no. But how 'bout we step

into the dining room and let us buy your supper and you can tell us all about it!" He took the preacher's arm and turned him toward the doorway to the hotel and dining room. Elly was at his side, Estrella following close behind, and they stepped back to let the preacher enter, then followed him into the building. The parson led them to a table near the front window, lifted his eyebrows in a question if the table was suitable and Reuben responded with a smile as he reached for a chair, pulling it out from the table for Elly to be seated and also seated Estrella.

As they scooted up to the table, Reuben began, "I'm sorry we didn't introduce our new addition, since we became the, well, I guess you could say, the guardians or parents of this young lady from the Santa Fe area. She is getting used to the busyness of the city, was fitted for a few dresses and her head is kind of in a tizzy." He smiled at Estrella, looked back to the preacher and paused as the waitress came to the table to take their order and quickly left.

"It is a pleasure to meet you, Estrella," replied the parson, looking at each of the three.

"So, how have you been Parson?" asked Reuben, smiling at their friend.

The Reverend smiled, dropped his eyes, "Winter was a bit challenging, made several trips over Mosquito pass by snowshoe, carrying mail and dust, held services on both sides of the pass and reached several men, but I'm glad the snow's melting and the mountains are green!"

"I don't know how you do it, Reverend," began Elly, reaching her hand out to touch his, "But you are an inspiration to many, especially us," nodding to Reuben.

"Thank you, my dear. The Lord's work is sometimes very difficult, but the rewards are immeasurable. But enough about me, I must tell you about today." He scooted his chair closer to the table and began, "I had just made the trip across Mosquito Pass with mail and packages from California Gulch. As usual, I took it to McLaughlin's Ranch, the stage station, I've stopped there often, stayed the night a few times, but ..." he shook his head as if to clear his mind and continued. "I had just left, but saw several men, five or six, riding up to the station as I rounded the corner of the barn. I didn't think anything of it, at first, but there was something familiar about one of the men. After I had ridden a mile or so, it just got to bothering me and I stopped, thought about it and turned back. But as I neared, I heard a gunshot, went to the edge of the trees and saw the stage sitting in front of the station and the men were moving about, waving pistols. I watched while they loaded their horses and rode off, then went to the station. I found the stage driver dead, Dan McLaughlin and McClelland tied up and gagged. They told me those men were 'Secesh', you know, Southern Sympathizers, secessionists. Dan heard 'em talking and thought they were expecting other Secesh in the park to join up with 'em."

"Did they get much?" asked Reuben.

"Well, I had delivered over a thousand dollars in gold dust, close to that in amalgam, and some cash in the letters. Dan said they got over four thousand in gold and maybe a thousand in greenbacks and gold coin, all that was waiting to be shipped out on the stage."

As they were speaking, Reuben saw someone come in the doorway, stop and look their direction. Sheriff Jack Sparks saw Reuben and immediately started for their table. He was obviously upset as he pushed his way through the tables and other diners. Reuben nodded, motioned to the empty chair and said, "Sheriff, join us?"

"Uh, yeah," he responded, looked at Elly and Estrella, doffed his hat and nodded, "Ladies." As he seated himself, he looked at the Reverend, "Father Dyer, how are you?"

"Fine Sheriff, you?"

"Madder'n a wet hen!" he looked at Reuben, "Them Rebs you spoke of, they done hit one of the stage stations, killed a couple men, stole everything of value and took off to the high country!"

Dyer frowned, "Two were killed? Are you sure? I only saw one!"

"You were there?" growled the sheriff.

"After it happened, yes. I deliver the mail and packages to McLaughlin's every time I cross the pass."

"McLaughlin's? I weren't talkin' 'bout Mac's place, it was the Witter station in Hamilton I was told about!" He paused, his brow furrowing and eyes blazing, "You mean to tell me they hit both stations?"

"I don't know about the other one, but they definitely hit McLaughlin's. Killed the driver and stole more'n five thousand in gold, greenbacks, and amalgam."

The sheriff glowered at Reuben, "So, now what?"

The parson looked from the sheriff to Reuben and frowned, glancing to Elly his facial expression formed the question and Elly smiled and looked to her husband as he began to answer, "Well, sheriff, you might want to raise a posse, or just ride up there and check it out, or..." and with a shrug, he lifted his coffee cup to take a sip, making it a little noisier that usual. He lowered the cup, glanced at the sheriff and said, "As for me and mine, we're going to have our meal, think about it, and then decide."

The sheriff sputtered and mumbled, "Just like ever' thang else that comes from that gov'nor! Them politicians ain't worth the powder it'd take to blow their nose!" He stood abruptly, pushed his chair in to the table, leaned on the back of the chair and glowered at Reuben, "Then I reckon ain't nuthin' gonna happen cuz that's outta my jurisdiction!" With a shake of his head, he stood, took a deep breath that made his moustache stand out from his face like the horns of a bull on the prod, hoisted his britches up to try to cover his paunch, turned and stomped from the dining room.

The parson shook his head, letting a slow grin split his face, until he could hold his laughter no more and began to snicker. The image of the sheriff and his horns of a moustache as he bounced out of the dining room was more than they could stand. The parson's stifled laughter prompted the others to loosen the dams of civility and within the moment, all four were laughing together. As the hilarity began to subside, they turned to the meal that had been set before them as they laughed, and began to eat, with short bursts of laughter interspersed between the courses.

The parson wiped his mouth, snickered again, and looked at Reuben with a sober expression, "Well, he did have a good question. What happens now?"

"I reckon I'll have to go after 'em, can't have a bunch o' outlaws runnin' around killin' folks. After all, this is not the battleground of the war, although they might want it to be so, it just can't be allowed."

The parson looked from Reuben to Elly, back to Reuben, "The way I saw it, and with what the sheriff said, there's more than just a few of them. Seems to me, the odds are against you."

"Well, pastor, isn't that the way it usually is, evil doesn't lack for numbers but good usually prevails in the end?"

"Yes, that is true, but many times it takes a while and

considerable cost for the good to prevail and usually, all too many have to pay the ultimate price for the good to prevail."

Reuben's eyes dropped to his plate, he sighed and looked up at the parson, "But for good to prevail, the forces of good must be willing to pay that price."

"Indeed, indeed," resolved the parson.

Elly and Estrella had remained quiet during the brief conversation until Elly said, "Well, my good man," leaning to bump shoulders with Reuben, "this time, you are *not* leaving me behind. *Whither thou goest, I will go ...and the Lord do so to me and more also, if ought but death part thee and me.* Wasn't that part of the vows we took when we were joined?" She smiled up at her man, pulling herself closer to him and resting her head on his shoulder.

Reuben grinned, looked at the parson, "What's a man to do when he's got a partner like this?"

The parson chuckled, "There just ain't no arguin' with a woman that has her heart set on something! She's just like my Harriet, God rest her soul."

Reuben looked from Elly to Estrella, "But, we have additional responsibilities," he started until the parson raised his hand to stop his protest.

Reverend Dyer looked at Estrella and asked, "Estrella, would you mind being put to work helping me set up for services? It's just a matter of arranging some chairs, maybe sweeping the floor, stuff like that. In exchange, I'll provide a stipend to take care of your meals and your room at the hotel, at least until these two," nodding to Reuben and Elly, "return."

Estrella looked at her friends, back to the parson, "If it is alright with Elly, I would be happy to help you," she answered, glancing from one to the other. She looked back to Elly, "But if you want me to go with you, you know I can use a rifle and will not hesitate to do so." Her eyebrows were lifted, accenting the question and offer of help.

Elly smiled, glanced from Reuben to Estrella, "I think it would be just fine for you to help the parson, Estrella. I'm sure it won't be for more than a few days, maybe a week or so," she glanced back to Reuben for confirmation of her estimation. He nodded, glanced back to the parson who nodded his agreement, and smiled at Estrella. Now he knew a little about how a parent felt the first time their offspring set off on their own.

13 / PURSUIT

Reuben strode from the Platte City Mercantile, arms full of supplies. Elly waited, leaning against the hitchrail where Blue, Elly's appaloosa, Daisy, and the pack mule were tethered. Bear lay at her feet but rose when Reuben exited the store. As Reuben stuffed the cornmeal, flour, sugar, pork belly, and more into the panniers, Elly rubbed Bear behind his ears, talking to him in low tones, occasionally glancing to her man as he loaded the mule. "Where's Estrella?" asked Elly, frowning as she looked at Reuben.

Reuben chuckled, "She's still inside, the young clerk in there was showing her some geegaws or something, I think he's taken with her and she's liking the attention!"

"And you left her in there?" asked Elly, standing up and looking toward the doorway.

"Uh, yeah, that's an emporium, not a tavern or somethin', ain't nothin' wrong with her flirting a little, as long as she, well, you know," stammered an embarrassed Reuben, realizing he wasn't thinking like a substitute father.

"Reuben!" grumbled Elly as she started for the doorway, but stopped as Estrella stepped out, followed by the young clerk. They were laughing and Estrella looked at Elly, wide-eyed but smiling.

"Oh, Elly, Johnathan here knows the Reverend Dyer and he's going to come to the dance hall where he's having his meeting and help us set up! Isn't that wonderful?" declared Estrella.

Elly paused, looking from Estrella to Johnathan and asked, "Have you been to Reverend Dyer's meetings before?" she asked, forcing herself to be calm and sound more pleasant than she felt.

"Yes ma'am, my family always goes to the preacher's meetings whenever he's in town."

"That's good to hear, Johnathan. And your father owns the Emporium?" asked Elly.

"Yes ma'am, we started the business almost three years ago. My father is considering putting in other stores in Buckskin and Breckenridge. If he does, he expects me to run one." The young man seemed to stand a little taller and smile a little broader, his pride showing a mite.

Elly glanced to Reuben, saw him grinning and chuckling as he finished packing the supplies and buckling them down. He looked at Elly, nodded toward the horses, "We need to get a move on!"

Elly stepped to Estrella, gave her a big hug and held her at arm's length as she looked at her, "We'll be back soon. Now you be careful and stay close to the reverend whenever you can." She looked up at Johnathan, "I will thank you to mind your manners with Estrella and do what you can to protect her. Can I count on you to be the gentleman your father raised you to be?"

"Of course, ma'am. I promise you I will spend as much time with Estrella as I can!" he replied, smiling broadly as he looked from Elly to Estrella, prompting the girl to drop her eyes as her neck and face showed a slight flush.

"Alright Estrella, and don't forget to pick up your outfits from the dressmaker." Estrella smiled, nodding happily, and waved to Reuben and Elly as she swung aboard the appaloosa and moved alongside Reuben. Both turned in their saddles to wave to Estrella and started from Front Street to make their way to the road to Hamilton and beyond.

"I never thought I would understand how my parents felt whenever I left the house to go anywhere without them." She shook her head, looking at Reuben, and added, "Makes me feel old!"

"Old? You're not a whole lot older than Estrella!" declared Reuben, chuckling as he looked at his wife whose head was hanging as she thought about the girl. "She'll be fine! That's a girl that has been a captive of the Apache and the Comanche and not only survived to tell the story but can hold her head high for what she endured and how she prevailed! The last thing that would be a threat to her safety would be some skinny little store clerk!"

"I suppose you're right. *But* we're responsible for her!"

"Ummhmm, but she's got to grow up and unless I miss my guess, she's already done that even while we were watching. I reckon that boy might be thinking of something a little more permanent. Did you see the way he puffed out his chest when he talked about running one of his father's stores?"

"Yes. But he's so young!" she pleaded, as if stating such a thought would make it real.

"He's probably older than you and you've been married a good while!" explained Reuben, grinning at his exasperated woman.

Elly looked at her man, shook her head and admitted, "I know, I know. I'm acting like an old woman or a mother hen protecting her one chick, but ..." she shrugged and nudged the appaloosa ahead of Reuben, twisting around in her saddle and laughing, "I'm takin' the lead this time!"

Elly was in the lead as they angled up the west side of Red Hill to cross over the long timbered ridge. As they crested, she reined up and stepped down, stretching her legs and enjoying the view. Before them and below the long ridge, a fertile valley that carried the trickling stream of Trout Creek through deep grass that moved in the wind like the waves of the ocean. Although Elly had never seen the ocean, she had seen the way the waves moved on big lakes and could only imagine what it would be like to stand on the deck of a big ship, moving with the wind and the waves, and watching the wonder of God's creation moving before them. A herd of Pronghorn Antelope grazed in the greenery, their tan coats and white rumps contrasted by the black horns of the bucks and smaller horns of the ewes, offered a scene of wonder seldom witnessed by the hordes of movers and prospectors that surged to the west. She breathed deep as she shaded her eyes to enjoy the cool breeze and the beauty of the Creator's handiwork. Reuben slipped up beside her and moved his arm around her waist and whispered, "It's a wonder, isn't it?"

"Ummhmmm, it certainly is and every time I see something new like this, I am amazed that anyone could deny the existence and power of Almighty God," replied Elly with a voice filled with wonder and awe. She dropped her eyes and turned to look at her man, putting her arms around his neck and clasping her hands behind him, "Thank you."

"For what?" asked a bewildered Reuben. Enjoying the closeness and solitude in the vast expanse of wonder.

"For rescuing me from the Indians and the wagon train. If you had not come, I would never have had this moment and the many wonderful moments He has already given us."

"That goes for both of us. You may not have rescued me from the Indians, but you rescued me from an aimless wandering life without purpose."

They embraced, clinging to one another in gratefulness until a yellow-bellied marmot mounted a big boulder nearby and sounded his whistle of alarm than sounded like someone was whistling at them. They pulled away, looking around, and Elly finally spotted the pot-bellied furry creature that looked like a big fat short-tailed squirrel and she pointed him out, laughing at the sight and their own reaction to such a varmint. Bear barked at him, and the furry creature disappeared in the rocks, leaving Bear barking and wagging his tail, looking from the big rock back to Elly.

"I think we need to get back on the trail, don'tchu?" she asked, mounting her appaloosa. Reuben swung aboard the roan and the wide trail allowed them to ride side by side, with Bear in the lead. They had traveled just over a couple miles from the crest of Red Hill until they came the crossing of Trout Creek where they met up with another rider coming from the Northeast.

The rider stopped, letting his horse get a drink as he

greeted Reuben and Elly. "Howdy folks! Travelin' far?" he asked.

"Don't really know," answered Reuben, "we're bound for McLaughlin's for now, probably go on to Hamilton and then ..." he shrugged as if they were just wandering and seeing the country.

The man kept looking up the wagon road that forked off the main road and said, "You might wanna be careful, there's brigands about."

Reuben frowned, "Whatchu mean?"

"I'm the closest thing this country has to a doctor, I'm Doc Cooper, more of a horse doctor really, but I was summoned by Adolphe Guiraud," nodding up the fork, "seems some men attacked his woman and she's in bad shape. I reckon it's the same ones that hit the stage stops and killed three men."

"I'm Reuben Grundy and this is my wife, Elly," replied Reuben.

"Pleased to meet you folks," answered the Doc, nodding to Elly as he touched his hat brim.

"When was this, Doc?" asked Elly.

"Yesterday mornin', ma'am. Bad thing, yes'm, it sure is. Well, I gotta get to the ranch house, see if I can do any good."

"I've done a little bandaging and such, perhaps I could be of help?" asked Elly.

The doctor frowned, looking at the young blonde woman, slowly nodded, "Perhaps it would be good to have a woman to help. Women folk always seem a little more comfortable with another woman around and in this country, they're in short supply. So, yes'm, I could use your help." He reined his mount toward the wagon road and Reuben and Elly followed close behind.

Reuben pushed his roan up beside the doctor's big

chestnut and said, "You know who did all this terrorizin'?"

"All I know is most folks think they were a bunch of Confederate renegades. We've had some trouble before, but nothin' like this, and I'm afraid this won't be the last of it."

"What makes you say that, Doc?"

"I dunno, maybe it's just a gut feelin' but things like this, when there's more'n one, there usually is a bunch before they get stopped. Now if it was just one hold up and nothin' more, then the outlaw or outlaws would have left the country with their bounty. But when there's more, in this case, three that I know of, I think there's gonna be more, perhaps a lot more. If they're true Confederates and not just a bunch of sympathizers takin' advantage of the times, then they'll try to get more of the gold shipments and anything else that would help the cause. But that's just my speculation, and what do I know, I'm just a horse doctor!" he grumbled.

They pulled up in front of the ranch house, which was a two-story structure, well-built and solid, made with big logs and extraordinary craftsmanship. The builder, Adolphe Guiraud, pushed open the front door, and motioned to the doctor to hurry. "C'mon Doc, she needs you somethin' awful!" With a quick glance to the others, he turned back into the house, "I'm comin'!" his words muffled by the interior of the home. The doctor quickly stepped down, handing off the reins to his mount to Reuben and motioned to Elly to join him. Both went quickly into the house, the doc packing his black bag.

Reuben stepped down and slapped the reins of the horses and mule to the hitchrail, loosened the girths and stretched before stepping into the house. It was a spacious home, especially for this part of the country where most homes are no more than a couple rooms, but this home was comparable to that found in the city. He doffed his hat and took a seat in a comfortable chair in the main room, listening to the bustle in the bedroom, and took a moment to say a quick prayer for the woman.

14 / RESOLVE

"She's awful bad, doc," shared Adolphe, tears in his eyes and he wrung his hands, looking toward the bedroom door that stood slightly ajar.

Doc Cooper knelt at the bedside and took the woman's hand to feel for the pulse in her wrist. He put a hand to the woman's forehead, checking for a temperature and was stunned at the bruises, bumps, and abrasions. One eye was black and swollen, the other closed with tears leaking out. Her breath was ragged, and she mumbled in misery, tossing her head side to side. One knee was drawn up and she kicked at the covers, "NO, NO," she shouted, then mumbled, "Please don't! No ... no ..."

Blood came from her mouth, a big abrasion covering her cheek and chin. Elly was on the far side of the bed, kneeling beside it as she took the woman's hand and began to talk to her softly. As she leaned toward the woman, she closed her eyes and began to pray. The woman, Martha Guiraud, calmed and quit fighting, listening to the voice of Elly. She struggled to open her one eye, saw Elly and tried to talk. Elly leaned closer, her ear near the woman's mouth as she listened to the faint voice, "He was a big man, smelly. God may forgive him, I can't." She struggled for another breath, "Adolphe knows them. Make the man pay!" she forced, turned to look at her husband and nodded, tried to smile and mouth the words, "I love ..." and breathed her last.

The doctor put his stethoscope to her chest, paused to listen a moment, then rose to his full height and looked down at the woman, as Elly closed the woman's eye and glanced to her husband. The big man dropped to his knees, reached for his wife's hand and began sobbing. The doctor motioned to Elly to come with him and leave the man with his wife. As they stepped through the doorway, the doctor quietly slipped the door closed and motioned to Reuben to join him outside.

"She's gone," declared the doctor, tying his bag behind the cantle of his saddle, looking at Reuben over his shoulder. "She talked with Elly, I didn't hear what was said, but there's no more I can do here, so I'll be leaving."

Elly stepped closer, looked at both the doctor and Reuben, "She said her husband knew the men. She said, 'Make that man pay!'" Elly shook her head, dabbed at a tear that fought to escape and looked away from the men. She breathed deep, thinking of the woman and what she suffered, and for that to be the last moments she had was a terrible thought. *No one should have to suffer that way!*

As the doctor stepped aboard his big chestnut, "I've got other patients, too many, but I have to try." He leaned on his pommel, looked at Elly, "Thank you for what you did, you gave that woman a bit of comfort. That means a lot."

The creaking of the opening door turned their attention to the front door of the ranch house to see the big Adolphe duck his head to come out. His tear-stained face and blood shot eyes told more than he wanted, but he looked at the doctor, "Thank you for coming Doc." He looked at Reuben, frowned, but looked at Elly, "And thank you, missy. I don't know your name but thank you."

Elly stepped forward, smiling to the big man and said, "I'm Elly Grundy, and this is my husband, Reuben," she motioned toward Reuben who stepped away from the horses and extended his hand to shake with the big man.

"I'm Adolphe Guiraud," he replied, shaking Reuben's hand, and dabbing at his tears with the other.

Elly stood beside the big man and asked, "Your wife said you knew the men who did this, is that right?"

Adolphe swallowed hard, nodded and growled, "I thought they were friends. Jim and John Reynolds and several men, maybe eight or ten, were with them. He said they were recruiting for the South. They tried that before when they were here prospecting when the war started." He shook his head, "I don't like the war and what it does, now this!" he nodded to the house and his wife, "but this had nothing to do with the war! This was … evil!" he spat, growling as he did, "If they come back, I will kill them with my hands!" he growled, slapping a fist into his palm.

"Do you know which one did this?" asked Reuben.

"The big man, Bobbitt I think his name was," he shook his head, breathing heavy as he tried to focus, "why?" he asked, frowning at Reuben.

Reuben pulled his Deputy Marshal badge from his pocket and showed the big man, "We're on their trail and there are about a dozen of 'em. It would be good to know which one has this way about him."

"My wife said to make him pay! If you don't get them, I will!" he declared, and turned and stomped back into the house.

Reuben tightened the girths on each of the animals and handed the reins of the appaloosa to Elly, offered her a helping hand which she ignored as she stepped into the stirrup and swung aboard. Reuben did likewise and they were soon on the road bound for the stage stops to see what else could be learned about the marauders.

Elly kind of liked being in the lead, Bear stayed closer to her, and it was just a short while when they rounded the timbered knob that marked the bend to Hamilton and showed the layout of McLaughlin's ranch and stage stop. As they took the road toward McLaughlin's, they spotted a small group standing atop a slight rise, heads bowed and gathered around what was obviously a grave. Elly reined up, waited for Reuben to come alongside and nodded to the hilltop, "Looks like a funeral."

"Must be for the driver that was killed," surmised Reuben. He motioned to the log building that had a fading sign over the door, *Stage Station*, "Let's wait there at the station. Maybe we can talk to McLaughlin. The preacher said he was a good man and would prob'ly be able to give us a little more information 'bout the rebels."

A stagecoach sat beside the station, no horses or mules harnessed, and it appeared the coach had been sitting a while. Reuben and Elly stepped down, tethered their animals at the hitchrail beside the building and stepped inside. They stood at the counter, their backs to the shelves of goods and leaned against the counter, waiting for the return of the station keeper. It was a brief moment when the doorway was filled with a gruff looking man holding a double-barreled coach gun and growled, "What'chu want?"

Reuben leaned forward, lifted his hands shoulder high and answered, "Whoa there friend. We're just looking to talk to McLaughlin. Is that you?"

"It is, and what do you want?" he grumbled, stepping into the room but still holding the coach gun on the two at the counter.

"I'm Reuben Grundy and this is my wife, Elly. I understand you were robbed by a band of Confederate guerrillas, is that right?"

"We was robbed, don't know if they was Confederates or not, 'though they talked like southerners. Kilt the driver, that was him we planted up thar on the hill and run off with gold and greenbacks. How's come you're int'rested?"

"We've been on their trail, want to put a stop to their marauding," stated Reuben as he brought his badge from his pocket to show the station keeper.

The man frowned, stepped closer for a better look at the badge, looked up at Reuben and over at Elly, and back to Reuben, "What kinda Marshal takes his wife on a manhunt with him!"

"I'm a deputy marshal also!" declared Elly, showing her badge pinned to her belt loop at her waist.

"Wal, if that don't beat all! A woman marshal, no wonder you ain't got nuthin' done!" declared the station keeper, walking around the end of the counter and placing the coach gun in the gun rack.

"Did you plant any of them rebels up there on the hill with that driver?"

"Uh, no."

"Then don't go criticizing me or us until I see your graveyard showing fresh dirt from plantin' outlaws!" spouted Elly, her frustration showing in her eyes.

The station keeper stepped back, bumping into his shelves and turning quickly to catch some cans that were rocking and starting to fall. He replaced the cans, turned to look rather sheepishly at the woman and said, "Pardon me ma'am, I guess I was just surprised about it is all."

Elly let a slow smile paint her face as she stepped to the counter and leaned her elbows on it and said, "Now, tell us what you can about the outlaws."

He started, "Wal, he said his name was Jim Reynolds and they ..." he continued his tale about him and the waiting passenger getting tied up, also the killing and the robbery. "They rode out in a hurry and best I could tell, they headed east along Tarryall Creek. Other'n that, can't really tell you much!"

"Do you know how many there were?" asked Reuben.

"Not rightly sure, there was two in here, one in the doorway, but he told that'n to get another'n to move the horses. Now the shotgunner said there was five of 'em, all told."

"Anything distinguishing about any of them or their horses?"

"Nope, they was just reg'lar lookin' fellas, 'ceptin' a couple of 'em had grey britches that looked kinda like uniform britches."

Reuben straightened up, glanced to Elly, "Well, we thank you. If you think of anything else, let the sheriff in Fairplay know."

"Won't do no good, all he says is it ain't his jurisdiction!" mumbled McLaughlin.

Reuben let Elly pass through the door and followed her into the open. They wordlessly stepped back aboard their horses and reined them around to start to Hamilton and the stage station that was also robbed.

The station at Hamilton was a picture of contradictions. With clapboard siding that had at one time been whitewashed, a sod roof, and a plank floor, it was unique in so many ways. Although it appeared like a normal dwelling, most with sod roofs had dirt floors, but because this was also a post office, the code required a plank floor because of the mail and packages. As Reuben followed Elly into the darker interior, the sunlight bent dusty rays through the two windows, while behind the counter stood a woman in a gingham dress, a full apron that contrasted the color covering her front, while a man stood slightly behind her, a coach gun's barrels resting on the counter, the man's hand on the grip and finger on the triggers.

The woman smiled at Elly, "How may I help you, ma'am?" she asked, glancing at Reuben and flashing a scowl to her husband who stood beside her.

"I take it you," nodding to the woman and to the man, "are the station keepers?" asked Elly, stepping close to the counter, giving only a passing glance to the man with the coach gun.

"Yes, we are. Were you wanting to take a stage or send something by mail?" she asked, glancing at Reuben and back to Elly.

"No, we're here about the robbery and killing that happened yesterday," started Elly.

The woman frowned, "Oh, and what would that be about?"

"We would like to know what happened, what you can tell us about those that robbed the station, anything like that," answered Elly.

"I don't understand, are you asking because you're concerned it may happen again?"

Reuben stepped forward and showed his badge, "No ma'am. We're on the trail of those men and the more we know might help us," he explained. "So, if you could tell us about it ..."

Mrs. Witter said, "Well, I don't know much. I saw the men riding up just as I was leaving to go into town. I did notice they were a rather rough looking bunch and the big one, he glared at me and snarled, licked his lips and nodded at me. I turned away, fearful though I was, and hurried on into town. I never thought they would do what they did. If I had, I ... well, Daniel can tell you the rest," she flustered, pulled out a hanky and fanned herself as she stepped back as if to give her husband room to talk.

The man stepped forward, took a deep breath and started, "There were three of 'em that came in and right off pulled a pistol on me and demanded the strongbox ..." he continued to recount the event, including the killing of the driver and shotgunner. "They said they were Confederates and didn't care about the law! I didn't see them shoot the two men, I was out cold," he touched the big knot on his head, bending to show Reuben the swollen bump and cut. "When I came to, they were long gone. Near as I could tell there were six of 'em."

"Did you or anyone give any kind of chase, follow the tracks or anything?" asked Reuben.

"Uh, no. I was pretty out of it with the head injury, an' my wife ran into town to tell the constable, but he couldn't or wouldn't do nothin'. He said that was a matter for the Volunteer Soldier boys."

"Well, I don't know if Lieutenant Shoup and his militia of volunteers will get involved or not, or if Sheriff Sparks will get a posse together, but for now, it's pretty well up to us," answered Reuben, nodding to Elly.

"You mean you two? You and the woman there?" asked the clerk, incredulous at the thought of a woman chasing after outlaws.

Elly just lifted her eyebrows, shook her head a little and turned away to go outside where the company of Bear and the horses was a little more tolerable. When Reuben joined her, he smiled and said, "Well, I reckon we take to their trail and see what happens!"

"Just us against a dozen murderin' outlaw rene-gades?" asked Elly.

"We've gone against greater odds. We'll just have to whittle 'em down a little," suggested a grinning Reuben.

———

"How'd ya do?" asked Jim, watching as John and his men stepped down from their mounts. They met about three miles from Hamilton, downstream on the Tarryall Creek. The wide streambed had carved its way across the flats, leaving a fertile green basin between two high banks that set apart about a quarter mile and stood almost a hundred fifty feet higher than the stream bottom. Their chosen meeting site was just below a bottle neck where the two banks pushed close together, separated by the willows, alders, and cattail bogs that covered about four hundred feet, providing excellent cover, especially with a lookout on the high point to watch for any pursuit.

"We got what I'd guess to be three thousand in gold, more in the mail pouch, and maybe a couple hundred from the station keeper. You?"

"I reckon we did 'bout the same, maybe a little more. The stage was carryin' some and the station had some. We'll wait till we camp for the night to get a better idea, but all in all, I think we had us a good payday!" He lifted his voice as he looked at the other men, "Don't you think so, fellas?"

"Yeehaw!" shouted Singletary and the others answered with hoots and hollers, slapping each other on the shoulder and laughing and chattering.

"Well men, we did good today, but every time won't be so good. But there's a couple other stations I want to hit, maybe some of these rich ranchers, and then we'll see what's left. We might work our way back to the diggings and hit some of the big mines."

"With nobody after us, it appears like we can do just about anything we want," declared Harvey Briggs, grinning at the brothers.

"Don't count on that happenin' very long. The more we hit, the madder they'll get and then they'll mount a posse or even get the militia involved. So, I suggest for now, we give the horses a break, let them graze and water, we'll have some coffee and somethin' to eat, then we'll head north to the mountains and find a better place to camp for a spell, kinda make it a base of operation."

They were in the upper end of South Park with the

towering snow-capped peaks of the mountain range that stood high above the park to the west, the timbered foothills to the north and east and the wide sprawling flats of the park to the south. All the boom towns of the gold rush lay against the mountains on the west but the foothills to the north were the last obstacle before the gold fields of the Gregory Diggings of Central City, Blackhawk, and Idaho Springs and ultimately, Denver City. The road from Denver City was constructed by the Denver, Auraria and South Park Road company in 1859 and had already seen a lot of travel with the gold rush of 1859 and the stage stations constructed along the way were tempting targets for the Confederate militia.

Jim let the men lay about for a couple hours before rousting them out to get ready to depart. "We're not that far from the road and all this flat country, it'd be too easy to see a big bunch like us, so, we'll split up, three groups. John will take one, Harvey one, and the rest will go with me. Let's get mounted," he ordered, picking Anderson Wilson, Addison Stowe and Jack Robinson to be his riding partners. He stepped aboard his mount and started to angle up the bank to ride across the grassy flat. With deep early summer grass that moved in the breeze like waves on a lake, tall bunches of sage that cast long shadows in the late afternoon light, and random bunches of Pronghorn antelope and mule deer, Jim was confident they could make the crossing unseen.

Dusk was cradling the sun in the western sky when the group came together near the headwaters of Snyder Creek. There was a ranch house just below the tree line, but the outbuildings were small, the corrals empty, and the house half dugout and half log did not speak of prosperity. Jim had decided to pass it by when the rest of the group gathered nearby. The creek bottom was thick with aspen and Jim took to the hillside to lead the band above the creek where the aspen met the ponderosa and offered passage on a dim game trail. John had come near and called out to his brother, "What'chu got in mind for a camp site for the night?"

Jim nodded to the upper reaches of the trail, "After we get atop the basin, there's a creek that cuts back to the west and makes a dogleg bend to the north. I figger we'll be outta sight there, able to have a cookfire and decent camp. Maybe tomorrow we'll come back down to hit the Kenosha house station just below the pass yonder," nodding to the west along the long timbered hillside.

"That'll also put us closer to the stations back toward Denver City too!" declared John, rocking in his saddle as his mount picked his way on the narrow trail, twisting among the pines and aspen.

"Ummhmm, Shaffer's Crossing, Junction, and Bailey are the one's I was thinking of, but, well, I'm not too sure. Those places have stations, but the gold comes from the Park and if we hit those stations, I'm not sure the others will have anything, 'ceptin' mail and such," surmised Jim, glancing back to his brother.

"What about hittin' some o' the bigger mines?"

"I dunno, they usually have too many men about 'em, some of 'em guardin' the ore, others just miners, and such. I was thinkin' about Oro City, California Gulch, or that way," nodding to the north, "the Gregory Diggings."

"Well, for now, how 'bout we find us a camp, get somethin' to eat, and get some sleep! I worked harder today than we did when we were placer minin'!"

16 / HUNT

Even though it had been a full day, six horses digging hooves as they're kicked into a gallop across soft-soil flats make a trail that even an eastern tenderfoot could follow. With Bear in the lead, Reuben and Elly rode side by side as the big black dog led them across the stage road and into the wide green creek bottom of the Tarryall Creek. The trail of the marauders bent away from the creek where the creek bed became a wide cat-tail strewn marsh. As the trail rode the shoulder of the south bank, they had gone no more than a mile from the road when the churned dirt of the outlaws' trail was joined by another bunch, appearing to be about an additional five riders. Reuben had stepped down to examine the tracks, saw a couple familiar hoof prints for each animal has his own distinguishing traits and when shod, even more unique, and looked up at Elly, "This is the bunch that hit McLaughlin's." He pointed to the east where the creek bent to the north and around a point of a bottleneck of the creek, "I'm guessin' they were just below that point, yonder."

"You don't think they're still there, do you?" asked

Elly, standing in her stirrups for a better look downstream.

"I doubt it, but we won't take any chances. Let's get up top there," nodding to the flat above the creek banks, "and we'll just be a couple looking for a place to build us a cabin."

Even though the tracks of the raiders fanned out and took three different ways, when they came from the creek bottom and all traveled the same trail, it was easy to see from the opposite bank. Reuben reined up, slipped his binoculars out of the saddle bags and stood in his stirrups to scan the flats between the creek bottom and the foothills to the north. "Far as I can tell, ain't nobody in the flats yonder, prob'ly already took to the mountains." He dropped the binoculars and looked at Elly, then to the creek below, "Let's cross over and take to the trail, but we won't follow directly. I reckon we need to make our own way so if any of 'em's watchin' it won't look like we're followin'."

As Reuben fidgeted with his binoculars, Elly nudged the appaloosa to the edge of the bank, looked over the edge and saw the steep slope but was certain the horses could easily make the descent. With a nudge of her heels, the appaloosa stepped over the edge and dug her hooves into the soft clay soil to work her way to the bottom. Reuben followed, trailing the mule and when he dropped into the green grass at the edge of the creek, he grinned at his woman, shook his head and said, "You're kinda likin' this leadin' the way, aren'tchu?!"

"I'm just a natural born leader, I guess," smirked Elly, fluffing her hair at her collar as she smiled coyly at her man. Bear barked and wagged his tail as he watched the two playfully banter with one another. They were soon across the creek and climbing the far bank when Bear stood at the top, looking down at the others and barked again, wagging his tail as if he was telling them to hurry.

———

THE LITTLE RANCH THAT SAT ASTRADDLE OF THE intermittent Snyder Creek showed little activity when Reuben and Elly drew near. Although the sun was cradled in the western mountains and long shadows stretched across the creek, they saw a woman with a sun bonnet and apron standing in the doorway, shading her eyes, as she watched them approach. When she saw the two and recognized one for a woman, the ranch wife smiled, "Welcome! Step down and make yourself t'home. I've got biscuits in the oven and a roast in the pot, and you're welcome to share!"

"Thank you!" declared Elly, nudging the appaloosa nearer before she reined up and stepped down. She walked closer to the woman, pushed her hat back to let it dangle by the chin strap and smiled, "It's mighty nice of you to invite us in, quite hospitable."

The woman stepped closer, "Oh, we so seldom get company, you're a sight for sore eyes. I'm Cordelia Matthews, and my husband, Otis, is in the barn." She looked to Reuben, "If you'd like to put your horses in the barn, you're welcome. My husband is feeding the stock and he'll point you to the stalls."

As she started to turn Elly smiled and said, "I'm Elly and my husband there is Reuben." The woman nodded, "It's nice to meet you," but shaded her eyes to look to the western horizon and smile, "The sunsets in this country are so beautiful!" she declared, causing Elly to turn and look. Brilliant shafts of gold stretched high in the heavens to fade into the darker blue that heralded the end of the day, while the lowering sun silhouetted the granite peaks and painted the bottoms of the few clouds with shades of gold, orange, and red. The Creator added a special touch as he outlined each of the clouds with a silvery gold lining, making each one stand-out from the fading blue of the evening sky.

"They are! I never tire of seeing the handiwork of our Creator," added Elly, also shading her eyes from the brilliance, yet both faces were bathed in the reflected glow of gold, giving each one an added touch of beauty. They smiled at each other, embracing the precious moment that bound them together and turned to go into the humble home.

The front room was warmed by the free-standing Spencer wood stove, with four burners, a small oven and a warming shelf below the oven and door. A big cast iron pot sat atop the stove and an enamel coffee pot was just off the burner plate and warming at the back of the stove. The table had two chairs sitting opposite one another, but Cordelia fetched two more chairs that were stacked in the corner and set them at the ends of the table. She motioned for Elly to take one and grabbed the coffee pot with her hand wrapped in the apron and turned to pour two cups full of steaming coffee. She replaced the pot on the stove, and quickly sat down, cornered away from Elly, smiled and said, "Now, tell me everything! We get company so seldom; the world could come to an end, and we wouldn't even know it!"

Elly chuckled, "First, let me ask you a question. We noticed several tracks of a good-sized group that rode past here, maybe a day ago, and I was wondering, did they stop?"

Cordelia frowned, "No, no, they didn't stop. We watched from the barn, and they were a motley looking bunch. One man, a big one, looked like the devil himself! Just the way he looked at the house and barn, like he was lookin' for somethin' or someone!" She shivered at the remembrance. "But they rode on by, they were talkin' a lot, motionin' to the house and barn, but the man in the lead barked at 'em and they all turned to listen to him. They kept goin' and I am certainly glad they did, too!"

"It's a good thing for you they did, they're the same bunch that held up two stage stations and murdered three people. They also stayed at the Guiraud ranch and attacked Mrs. Guiraud. She died this morning."

"Oh no! We've been to church with the Guirauds, she was a sweet woman. That's terrible, and Adolphe, he must be broken!" surmised Cordelia. She dropped her eyes, then lifted and looked at Elly as she frowned, "But, how do you know they're the ones?"

"We've been following them. They're Confederates, maybe soldiers or militia, but I think they're renegades and are just using the war as an excuse for raiding and stealing."

"Oh, that's a shame!" declared Cordelia, reaching for her cup.

The ladies continued talking about everything of mutual interest, events, clothes, frontier life, husbands and more, until they heard the men coming from the barn then jumped up and finished the last preparations for the evening meal. When the men entered, the women stood side by side, smiling like cohorts in a conspiracy, and offered chairs to the men and began serving the meal. Elly poured the coffee as Cordelia began dishing up the meat and vegetables onto the tin plates. When everyone was served, they joined hands as Otis bowed his head to pray. When the 'Amens' were said, the talk resumed as if the four were old friends and the conversation continued into the night.

The back room was separated by a rope holding two blankets and the Matthews' bed was behind the curtain. They made a palette on the floor of the front room for their guests. Bear stayed in the barn with his best friends, Blue and Dixie, and the night passed peaceably. When the first light of morning bent through the two windows of the front room, Reuben rolled out and went to the barn to check on the animals and to spend his time with the Lord. He had just said his Amen when Otis pushed open the big door and called, "Reuben, you in here?"

"No, I'm over here!" he answered. He had spent his morning time sitting on the top rail of the pole corral, enjoying the slow approach of the new day as the sun began to show its colors of red and pink dancing across the scattered clouds of morning.

"Oh, well, you're an early riser!" declared Otis, reaching for his pitchfork to throw some hay to the milk cow before he accepted her morning offering, howbeit begrudgingly.

"How long have you been here, Otis?" asked Reuben, leaning against the barn wall as Otis did the milking.

"Well, we came out in '60, tried the prospectin' but didn't know enough to do any good. Saw this piece of land and fell in love with it and we looked at each other and smiled, hugged, and threw away the pans for placer minin' and started cutting sod for the beginnings of our home. Knew right off that if we could grow vegetables and such, we could make more money digging vegetables from the dirt than we could huntin' for gold, and we've done alright. Ain't gettin' rich, but we're eatin' reg'lar." He stood, arched his back and groaned, then with a broad grin, "And we've raised some beef cows, sold 'em for 'most as much as gold! Raisin' some more and if this gold rush keeps goin', we'll have us a nice place. Maybe even get some store-bought goods for the missus."

After a quick breakfast of biscuits and gravy, Reuben and Elly said their goodbyes and started up the same trail taken by the rebels. With a wave to the Matthews, they turned back to their task. The silence followed them as both had their own thoughts about their new friends and the home they were building, and about their own future that held only a simple cabin in the Wet Mountain valley, far from here.

"I'd like to have a garden!" declared Elly, her spoken thought breaking the silence.

"What'd you say?" called Reuben from behind her. She was leading the way while he followed and trailed the pack mule. The horses were picking their way along the game trail that twisted about in the aspen thickets, the quaking leaves rattling in the morning breeze.

"I said I'd like to have a garden!" she answered, turning around in her saddle to look back at Reuben.

"Too late to have one this year. We'd had to plant it 'fore we left! We don't even know when we'll be getting back!"

She turned around in her saddle, saw they were approaching the edge of the trees and reined up. Before them stretched a wide grassy park with a large marsh at the upper end. The hills to the west were heavily timbered, while the smaller buttes on the east held both aspen and pine. Reuben pushed past Elly, stepped down and walked to the edge of the trees. The trail of the rebels continued across the park, appearing to go to the west of the marsh. At the west edge on the shoulder of the foothills lay the wagon road that carried freighters and stages to and from South Park and Denver City and places north. The creek bed that had carried Snyder Creek held nothing but a trickle although the tracks of the rebels followed the creek bed instead of the roadway.

Reuben turned back to Elly, "It looks like they're avoiding the wagon road, prob'ly lookin' for a place to make camp."

Reuben looked around, stepped from the trees for a better look at the ridge that rose to his right. It was thick with pine and aspen and was about a hundred feet higher than the road. He nodded to himself, turned back to Elly, "I think we'll make us a camp up yonder on the hill, back in the trees, so we can keep watch on what the rebels might be doin'. I'm not real anxious to run into 'em unprepared!" He stepped back aboard Blue, nudged him forward and pulled the lead to the mule taut and started into the trees to make their way to the crest of the ridge and find a likely promontory and camp.

17 / KENOSHA

"Who do ya' s'pose they are?" asked Rupert, motioning toward a group of riders coming up the road toward the station. Rupert Murdock was the shotgunner of the Hinkley & Co. stage that had come from Buckskin by way of Alma, Fairplay, and Hamilton to stop at the Kenosha House station. They had their first change of teams at Hamilton and Kenosha was their nooning stop and second team change. The Kenosha house sat on the shoulder of the big timbered hill that marked the last climb over Kenosha pass.

"Dunno, but after what we heard 'bout McLaughlin's and Hamilton, we might wanna be ready!" suggested Abner Williamson, the Jehu or driver of the stage. They had been helping the hostlers as they changed the teams. The three passengers were inside the station, taking their meal and tending to personal necessities as the Jehu and Messenger tended to the coach. They would get their meal on the run to save time.

Ab looked at Rupert, chuckling, "Maybe ol' Berry had the right idea!" he commented as they watched the approach of the handful of riders.

"You mean that mousy passenger?" asked Rupert, thinking of the small man with high water britches, a tattered jacket and three-day old whiskers. They knew the prospector from other trips when he took his dust into Denver City to deposit in the bank, refusing to trust the stage companies or anyone else with his hard-earned profits. "What'd he do?"

Ab chuckled, "Didn't you see him go into the barn?"

"Yeah, but I just figgered the outhouse was full!"

"Nah, he took his gold dust, buried it under the horse manure. I seen him do it 'fore, an' he usually makes it to the bank with his dust, smelly though it might be!" chuckled Ab, as he nodded with a somber expression to the riders as they pulled up in front of the station.

Ab turned to the hostlers, "Get a hurry on there fellas, I'm thinkin' we'll be needin' to haul outta here real quick like." He looked at the riders, saw two step up on the covered porch and start into the station, but three others had stepped down, slapping reins around the hitchrail and turned to the barn and stage. They walked toward the stage, ambling as if there was no concern or hurry, but the expression on their faces and their rumpled appearance set Ab and Rupert on edge. Ab asked Rupert in a low voice, "Your shotgun handy?"

"Nope. It's up yonder, in the boot."

"Ain't got no sidearm either, do ya?"

"Nope."

"Me neither," resolved Ab.

"You the driver?" asked the first of the three men. His appearance was little different than the others except his floppy felt hat was pinned up over his forehead with a gold-colored star shaped pin. There was nothing else that gave the appearance of a uniform, but the men were well armed, each one having a holstered pistol, another in their belt, and loosely carried a Springfield rifle like both the confederate and union forces had been issued.

"I'm the driver," replied Abner.

"Then climb on up there and throw down that strongbox!" declared the man, Harvey Briggs, "and don't go touchin' that coach gun I see sittin' up thar."

Ab started to protest, but both Harvey Briggs and the man beside him, Addison Stowe, had pulled their pistols and held them on both the driver and the shotgunner. Ab nodded, turned away and stepped on the footrest, then the hub of the front wheel, atop the wheel, and into the boot. He dropped on the seat, bent over and struggled with the heavy strongbox, but managed to pull it up, and tumble it over the side to crash to the ground beside the wheel.

Briggs looked at the driver, "Now, get on down here an' open it!" he snarled, waving his pistol at the driver.

Addison Stowe motioned to the shotgunner, "Get them hostlers back here an' unhitch them mules!"

"But that's a fresh team!" protested Rupert.

"Do it!" demanded Stowe, motioning with his pistol for the shotgunner to do as he was told. The third man, Owen Singletary, had stepped up beside Stowe and brandished his pistol in a similar manner, but he was grinning as he watched the two men. It wasn't often he had the opportunity or ability to force his way on others, since he was not a sizable man, and the chance to exert his will over others gave him a bit of a thrill.

Rupert grumbled, shaking his head as he started toward the barn, but stopped and hollered, "Hey you two! Git on back here!" he demanded as he reached down to unhook the trace tug chains from the single tree. The hostlers soon joined him and at the sight of the gunmen, quickly set to work to unhook the teams and take them to the barn.

Harvey Briggs turned back to the driver, "You, empty your pockets!"

"Empty my pockets? What for, I ain't got nothin'! I ain't never heard of a stage driver bein' accused of havin' any money!" he protested as he turned his pockets inside out to show the truth of his remark.

As the hostlers started away with the teams, Stowe demanded, "Bring back an axe, sledge, crowbar, anything like that and be quick about it!"

————

JIM REYNOLDS AND ANDERSON WILSON WALKED INTO THE log station, removing their hats as they stepped inside. They paused a moment, letting their eyes get used to the dim light, spotted the passengers seated at the long table, eating their noon meal. George Harriman was leaning against the counter at the side of the big room, watching his wife dish up the stew on the tin plates to the passengers. He looked at the newcomers, "You fellas wantin' to take a meal are ya?"

"That'd be fine," replied Jim Reynolds, stepping toward the table to find a seat on the long bench. He motioned to Anderson to sit beside him, and they hung their hats on the hooks beside the table before sitting.

Mrs. Harriman smiled, turned to her husband, "Fetch me the fixin's!"

Harriman brought the plates, cups and forks, sat them on the table and returned with the coffee pot to fill the cups as his wife dished up the stew. He looked at the two newcomers, "That'll be a dollar each!"

"A dollar!?" asked a surprised Jim Reynolds as he twisted to look at Harriman.

"That's right. Things are expensive up here in the high country!"

"We wanted to get some supplies too, an' we got a couple others that'll be in shortly. 'Sallright if'n we pay up when we're finished?" asked Jim, reaching for the fork.

"I reckon," replied Harriman.

The passengers had finished their meal, even to the wiping of the plates with the last of their biscuit to get all the gravy and thirstily poured down the coffee as they sat back to lean against the outer wall. One man dug out the makings for his pipe, tamped down the tobacco and struck a lucifer to light it, took a deep draw and blew out the cloud of smoke across the table. Jim Reynolds frowned at the man and turned his attention back to finishing his meal.

A sudden commotion of banging and breaking of wood came from the yard in front of the barn and Harriman stepped to the window to look out. He bent forward, wiped at the fly specked glass and muttered, "What the ..."

"What's the matter," asked William Berry, one of the passengers.

"They're breakin' up the stage! They can't do that!" he declared, reaching for the rifle that hung above the doorway.

"Don't do that!" declared a voice behind him that was accented by the clicking of a hammer on the pistol in his hand. Another click sounded as Anderson did the same. Both men were now standing, Jim with his pistol on the station keeper, Anderson with his on the passengers. Jim added, "Now, empty your cash drawer and your pockets, right there on the counter."

Anderson added, "And you three, empty your pockets on the table there."

Jim glanced to Mrs. Harriman, "Ma'am, I suggest you set three more plates for the rest of my men. They're almighty hungry! You see, robbing stages and stations is such hard work!" he chuckled as he waved his pistol at the station keeper. "Now, get me the strongbox from under your counter there," motioning to the counter.

"There ain't nothin' in there, we done put it in the strongbox on the stage," replied Harriman.

"Lemme see it anyway!" ordered Reynolds. Harriman bent to the box, set it on the counter and opened the lid to show it was empty. "Alright, put it away," directed Jim. He motioned to the greenbacks, coin, and the single leather pouch on the counter, "Put that in a bag," he ordered, "then take it to the table and add their things," motioning to the table where the passengers stood, hands raised.

"WHOOEEE!" shouted Harvey Briggs as he pushed through the door. "We got us a good bunch of gold from that strongbox. Driver said it was the takin's from Michigan Creek and Jefferson Creek! And it's a bunch!" He stopped, looking around at the men with their hands high, the station keeper putting the money in the bag, and then to Jim Reynolds. He lifted his eyebrows and shoulders as if asking a question.

"Call the others to get in here and get somethin' to eat," ordered Jim, "but have 'em bring in the others. We'll tie 'em up 'fore we leave."

Harvey nodded, turned to step out on the porch and holler the orders to the others. He came back in and took a seat at the table, pulling the cup of coffee closer as he smiled at Mrs. Harriman. He looked at Anderson, lowered his voice, "Good thing Bobbitt ain't with us, he'd take after that'n like a bear after honey!" Anderson frowned, glancing from Harvey to Jim, shaking his head slightly to suggest that Jim did not know about Bobbitt's behavior at the Guiraud's ranch. Harvey nodded and turned his attention to the food just as Addison and Owen came in behind the driver and shotgunner, pistols in their backs. After tying up the two men, they started to join Harvey at the table, but Jim stopped them, "Those too!" he ordered, pointing to the three passengers.

They quickly finished the task of binding the captives, and jumped to the table, eager to finish up the stew from Mrs. Harriman's pot. With a platter full of fresh hot biscuits, the men were quick to clean their plates and step away from the table, each one profusely complimenting and thanking the woman, who nodded and started cleaning off the table. Harvey looked to Jim, motioning to the woman and Jim nodded, "Yeah, she needs to be tied up too, otherwise she'll just let them," nodding to the bound and gagged passengers and others, "loose and they'll be after us 'fore we can get away. But, use her apron and don't gag her," he directed, nodding to the woman.

"Ma'am, let's just sit you down on this hyar chair and I'll tie your hands behind you. That way, you can be comfortable and not hafta suffer like them," directed Harvey, motioning to the chair at the end of the table. She obeyed and he quickly bound her hands together with her apron strings, "That ain't too tight is it ma'am?" he asked, to which she responded by shaking her head, her fear taking her willingness to talk away.

With a last check around, Jim asked Harvey, "What'd you do with the hostlers?"

"Same as them," nodding to the others that lined the wall, seated on the floor, hands bound behind their backs and their ankles bound.

"Then let's get outta here!" he ordered, waving his pistol to the others, letting them leave before him and closing the door behind him. They quickly mounted, and with bulging saddle bags, took off up Kenosha pass toward their camp on Geneva Gulch.

18 / SURVEILLANCE

T he morning sun was still lying low behind the tall granite tipped ridge of the Platte River Mountains that sided the North Fork of the South Platte and stood between Reuben and the rising sun. The mountains were thick with spruce, fir, and pine, interspersed with patches of quakies that added their light green leaves and white barked trunks to the dark greens of the high country. Reuben had climbed the lower ridge that stood above their camp and afforded him a view of the wide park that carried the wagon road from South Park to Denver City, the same road that had been traveled by the band of rebels and as Reuben suspicioned, who had made their camp somewhere in the many gulches, valleys and hills of this wild country.

He had already enjoyed his time with his Lord and thumbed through a few pages of Scripture, but a low growl from Bear brought his attention to the valley below. At its widest point, the flat-bottomed valley was just over two hundred yards wide, the road staying near the tree line on the far side, and six mounted men rode two abreast, with one man in the lead, his horse a couple paces ahead of the rest. Reuben chuckled, remembering the way of many officers and others that always had to show what they perceived as their superiority, whether by position, clothing, or attitude, and such was the man aboard the big black. With no pack animals or wagons, it was evident these were not gold hunters, at least not the working kind. Reuben lifted his binoculars and brought them into focus. Although he had never seen the rebels close-up, he recognized them by descriptions given, clothing worn and bits of uniforms showing.

As he watched, the group slowed, the leader motioning to the big man beside him, and the lone man peeled off from the band, and started across the flat toward the trees below the ridge of Reuben's promontory. Reuben frowned, watching the others continue south on the road, but perplexed by the one that separated from the others, until the man reined up before entering the trees and slipped his rifle from the scabbard that hung from the pommel in front of his right leg. The rifle sat in the scabbard, muzzle down, and the big man lifted it up, lay it across his pommel to check the load before starting into the trees. *Must be doin' some huntin' for meat for the bunch,* thought Reuben.

He watched the man disappear into the trees before looking down to Bear, motioning toward the camp below them, "Go Bear, go to Elly! Now!"

The big dog rose, started away, looked back at Reuben and turned to trot back through the trees to return to camp. He knew the dog would immediately go to Elly's side, and also knew Elly would be busy fixing their breakfast. He was confident she would keep her rifle nearby and that she was never without her Colt Pocket pistol in the holster on her hip, usually obscured by the buckskin jacket.

He was concerned about the confederate rebels. The group that passed by was just half of the bunch, which meant the rest were probably on their way to a different stage station or other possible target that would hold riches for the renegades. He and Elly had been through this country before when they first came to South Park, had traveled the road that came from Denver City to South Park. As he thought of the area, he remembered there were many gulches that carried spring runoff to the river and offered several sites for an outlaw camp, but the closest to his position was the Hoosier gulch, followed by the North Fork branch and then the Geneva gulch. And if the other bunch was going after another stage station, it would be the Bailey Ranch or Junction Station. He shook his head, uncertain of what they would do, and wishing there was some way he could cover both, but he couldn't arrest anyone without knowing for sure what had been done and what they might be planning. He made another quick scan of the valley and the road before rising and replacing his binoculars and picking up his rifle to start back to camp.

"BOBBITT, I WANT YOU TO SPLIT OFF HERE, DO A LITTLE huntin' and see if you can get us some camp meat. A nice sized deer, maybe an elk, somethin' we can sink our teeth into. Think you can do that?" asked Jim Reynolds, looking at the big man that rode to his left.

"Yeah, I can do that. Did a bit o' huntin' back ta' home. Always managed to bring home the meat," answered the big man, reining his plow horse sized bay gelding away from the road. With a wave over his shoulder, he started away.

"Hold up a minute!" hollered Reynolds, "We're not goin' to be long at the station, and we'll be comin' back this same way. John and the others went downriver to see 'bout takin' either Bailey's or Junction, an' they'll be comin' back too. So, try to get us somethin' and get back to camp so we can have some meat for a big meal."

"Yeah, yeah," grumbled the big man, diggin' his heels into the stubborn bay. He pointed the horse to swing wide of the marsh and start for the aspen that hugged the west flank of a long ridge. He knew elk liked to bed down in the aspen and it was still early, and he might kick some out of their beds. He glanced back at the bunch of riders with Reynolds, turned to look at the aspen, and reined up, cocking his head to the side and squinting his eyes to sort out what he was seeing. With the sun rising beyond the tall ridge and mountains, the light caught the thin wisp of rising smoke that came from high up on the lower ridge, near where the aspen gave way to the black timber. The smoke was slightly dissipated by the pines, but with no breeze in the early morning and the angle of the rising sun, it was as if the light was focused on the little bit of smoke that had to come from a campfire.

Bobbitt grinned, thinking, *Why go to the trouble of huntin' when I can just take what I want from some dumb prospectors!* He chuckled to himself and nudged his mount forward to take cover in the aspen. For such a big man, Bobbitt was an experienced woodsman and moved silently through the trees. He had tethered his mount in a thicket of aspen and took to the edge of the pines, using the darker cover to his advantage and with a carpet of pine needles, he could move as quietly as the shadows he used for cover.

Elly heard the whisper of pine branch against material and tensed. She was on one knee beside the fire, her hand on the frying pan as she watched the bacon sizzle in the grease. She slowly rose, slipping her hand inside her jacket to clasp the butt of the Colt, glanced to her Henry that leaned against the big flat rock with the rest of the morning fixings. The coffee pot danced on the rock as the flames licked at its side, and Elly moved a little closer to the Henry. She bent to move the coffee pot back when a gravelly voice sounded, "Well lookee here! Ain't this sumpin'!"

Elly looked up, wide-eyed, at the big man. Black whiskers covered his face, heavy eyebrows did little to cover his black eyes, and his floppy felt hat was cocked to the side. The man wore wool britches held up by wide galluses that stretched over his massive frame covered by a red and black plaid wool shirt that fought bone buttons that stretched the fabric to its limit. High topped lace-up boots looked to be the size of grizzly paws and the big arms had ham-hock sized paws that flexed as he neared. A Springfield rifle was cradled under one arm, but the big figure made the rifle look like a piece of kindling wood. Rotten teeth showed from behind the whiskers as the man growled, "Where's your man?" and cackled as he slowly came closer.

"He's coming back for his breakfast any minute now!" stated Elly, trying to sound confident and unafraid, rising to full height which was still miniscule compared to the big man. She grasped the pistol butt, keeping her hand inside the jacket and turning three quarters to the man, glancing to the trees that held the game trail used by Reuben to go to the mountain top.

When she looked away, Bobbitt lunged, catching her off balance, and the weight of the big man bore them both to the ground, but Elly held tight to the pistol, dragging it from the holster as she stumbled away from the man, but his weight bore down on her as she tried to cock the hammer, catching her thumb and pinning it tight to her side. Bobbitt buried his face against her neck, growling as his paws reached for her arms, but another growl and black fur flashed at the side as Bear launched himself at the attacker.

Bear sunk his teeth in the neck of the monster eliciting a scream from the man as he reached for the attacking beast. His move loosened Elly's pinned hand and she brought the Colt to full cock, twisted the muzzle away from her and pushed it against the belly of the big man, dropping the hammer in a muffled roar that sent the .36 caliber slug into the man's lower stomach, just below his belt buckle. Bobbitt screamed as Bear sunk his teeth further in the man's neck, growling and snarling all the while, and when the Colt roared, Bobbitt realized he had been shot and pushed up from the woman, swatting at the attacking dog.

Elly eared back the hammer again and shot again. The flame from the muzzle singed his shirt, smoke puffed and burnt his eyes, and the bullet bore through his massive gut, striking the man's spine and driving through. Bobbitt was dead and did not know it; still growling at the black dog, trying to swat it away. He tried to take a deep breath but brought only blood that he spat to the side. Elly shot again, the bullet crashing through the man's solar plexus and splitting as it penetrated his mass, bearing the messenger of death that finally rendered the man his due. Bobbitt growled, looked down at Elly, blood streaming from his mouth and front, choked on the blood and fell to the side, eyes staring at the rising sun that bent a golden shaft of light through the tall pines.

Reuben ran from the trees, rifle in hand and held at the ready, saw the big man, Bear now astride of the form, and Elly crawling away. He ran to her side to kick the carcass of the monster away and call Bear off. He reached for Elly, lifted her to her feet, "Are you alright?"

She nodded, shaking her head, weak-kneed, she leaned her face against his chest and said, "I think breakfast is ready!"

19 / SCOUT

They were packed and mounted, ready to leave the camp, cross over the ridge and take to the bench park that sat high above the valley with the wagon road, but through the quakies he spotted several riders coming up from the Park on the Kenosha wagon road. He stood in his stirrups, bending and twisting to see through the trees and recognized the riders, he glanced to Elly, "It's the same riders that'n," nodding to the body of Bobbitt, "came from, the same bunch we been trackin'. I'm guessin' they hit either the Kenosha station or maybe raided the prospectors up Guernsey, Deadman, or Michigan Creek or thereabouts." He paused, watching the riders, "But if I had to put money on it, I'd say they took the station."

Elly also watched the riders, having a better view through a break in the trees and responded to Reuben, "What're we gonna do?"

"What we already planned. We'll cross over, through the trees and take to that bench. The wagon road there makes a big bend around the point of the ridge, and this way will save us some time and maybe get there before them. I'm sure the other end of this bench will overlook the wagon road where it follows the South Platte and probably give us a better look at where they might be camped." He dropped into his saddle, reined Blue around and started through the trees, trailing the mule and followed close by Elly.

The bench was a shoulder across the west end of the long ridge that separated South Park from the North Fork of the South Platte River. Below the ridge at the west end was the wagon road and the gulch that carried the feeder creeks to the South Platte, while above the bench rose the Twin Cone Peaks that stretched above timberline to show their granite tips. Once on the grassy bench, Reuben twisted around and motioned Elly alongside and as she neared, he pointed out to the creek in the bottom of the bench, "That's the Kenosha Creek that works its way down to the confluence with the South Platte. I'm thinkin' those outlaws have their camp back up in one of those gulches that feeds the Platte. We should reach that canyon of the Platte before they do, and maybe we can get a looksee as to where they're hidin' out."

Elly huffed, "Then what? You expect us to round up the whole bunch?" she asked, skeptically.

"No, but if we know where they are, maybe we'll get an opportunity or two that might whittle 'em down a mite," he grinned and chuckled as he turned to face her.

The grassy bench appeared as a flat-bottomed valley with the Kenosha Creek, lined with willows and alders, wound its way through the two miles of scattered timber. From his previous promontory, Reuben saw the valley was a slash across the shoulder of the high ridge, making a straight-thru short-cut to the wagon trail traveled by the rebels. As they approached the north end, the tall firs and spruce pushed in from the flanks of the ridge, marking the end of the bench, but the creek tumbled down through the trees to join the other feeder creeks that came from the high country. Reuben reined up, pointed to the rocky promontory above them to the right, "I think I'll go up there and take a look see," and stepped down.

Elly followed his lead and swung down beside her appaloosa, looking around until Bear growled and went into his attack stance, looking into the thick timber, dark with shadows. Elly went to the other side of her mount, slipped out the Henry and watched as Reuben did the same. Reuben's first thought when he saw a batch of dark fur was a grizzly bear, but a big nose and two big ears came from the shadows. He whispered, "I think it's a moose!"

Elly giggled, "No, it's three moose! Can't you see the little ones?" she pointed with the muzzle of her Henry. As the long-legged gangly cow moose came from the water at the back water pool of the creek, something green hung from one ear as she stopped and looked at the intruders to her domain. Beside her stood two calves, no more than a couple weeks old, wide-eyed and curious at the creatures standing before them. When Bear saw the calves, he dropped to his belly, tail wagging, and looked as if he wanted to play. Elly nodded to the dog, "Look at him! What kind of protector is that?" she asked, laughing.

But the moose had a different idea of what was going on and laid back her ears and feigned a charge at the intruders. She stopped, looked back at her calves and turned to face Reuben and Elly. Reuben said, "She's blocking the break in the trees with the trail! I need to get up there before the outlaws get here!"

"Well, go ahead and give it a try! I dare ya!" giggled Elly, watching the mother guard her calves, "But I don't really think it's a good idea!" As she spoke, the cow made another charge, trying to drive the intruders away and all three backed up closer to the horses.

Reuben reached for the reins on Blue and without taking his eyes off the cow, told Elly, "Get ahold of your horse, let's back away and give her room."

They backed away from the edge of the willows, moving closer to the black timber, but always watching the cow. The moose was taller at the shoulder than either of the horses and the horses were getting a little skittish as they watched, wide-eyed, ears pricked, snorting and side-stepping all the way. The big cow grunted, sounding like she was grating her teeth, and one of the calves squealed at its mom. Blue stopped, shook his head as if taunting the cow, laid his ears back and stretched out his head and neck, digging at the dirt with his front feet like he was ready to do battle with the cow, but Reuben jerked on the rein and spoke to him, "Easy boy, you don't want to get in a fight with her, she's bigger'n you!" and backed closer to the trees.

Finally, the cow, believing she had gotten the better of the intruders, turned back to her calves, grunted and groaned at them, and the three trotted upstream without a look back at the group. Reuben shook his head, laughed and looked at Elly who stood smiling as she watched the cow and calves trot away, "They say moose meat is good eating!"

"You wouldn't dare! That's a momma and her young'uns! You'd never do that, would you?" asked Elly.

"Of course not, but the look on your face said you thought I would!" he chuckled. With a glance at the retreating moose, he reached for his binoculars and nodded to the trees, "I'm headin' up there. You might want to look for a possible camp site. Dependin' on what them rebels do, we might need to stick around here for a while."

She smiled, waved him away, and watched as he disappeared into the trees. He had motioned to Bear to stay with Elly and the big dog lay at her feet as she sat down next to a tall spruce, and ground tied the animals, letting them enjoy the tall grass.

Reuben stretched his longs legs out as he cut through the aspen, twisting through the thick growth of the white-barked trees. It was difficult to move quietly with the many branches that had fallen to the ground, probably from a recent high wind, but the matted leaves from the previous winter snowfall offered an alternative. As he passed through the aspen, the trail to the lower shoulder cut just below the rocky escarpment and to the edge of the slide rock, giving him a narrow trail to the point atop the big rock formation. He bellied down and slipped the field glasses from the case, gave the road a quick look before lifting the glasses. He placed his hat over the top of the glasses, protecting the lenses from the sun and any possible reflection that would give away his position, and began to search the canyon road.

As he moved the glasses back the direction where he expected to see the outlaws coming, there was nothing. He twisted around so he could look to the northeast, downstream on the Platte, but again, the road was empty. He shook his head, took a deep breath, and began to search for any place the riders might have left the road. Directly below his position, and for a good distance both ways, there was no place anyone would choose to leave the road. The steep bank on the far side was too steep and rocky, and this side held the river and thick timber. He gave it another long look, saw no sign of riders or trails leaving the road, and crabbed back from the point to re-case the binoculars and start back to Elly.

"We're gonna take to the road, see if we can find where they left it, if they did."

They were soon across the creek and on the wagon road, turned to the north siding the long ridge and paralleling the river. Reuben casually searched the edges of the road for any sign of riders coming or going. It was less than two miles before they neared the first gulch that came from the north carrying the headwaters of the North Fork. They dropped from the road, crossed the narrow river that was no more than fifteen feet wide and maybe a foot deep, pushed through the willows and scanned the bald faces of the many finger ridges that held scattered ponderosa interspersed with fir and spruce mostly on the west faces, searching for any sign of the band of confederate guerrillas. A two-track trail led from the road going upstream to the headwaters of the Platte, but it showed no sign of recent riders. Then just past the junction of the two roads, what appeared to be a recent trail angled off the road and took to a dry gulch between two ridges. The point of the taller butte was thick with rock formations with a few scraggly piñons holding tenuously to cracks filled with drifted soil. Left of the taller butte, a smaller butte, also with rimrock formations but not as big, stood as the lesser of the sentinels to the trail that took to the gulley between.

With a quick glance around for any visitors, Reuben pushed closer to the tracks, dropped to the ground and examined the sign. As he fingered the tracks he spoke, "These are all fresh this morning, and only about five or six horses, coming down off the hills there," nodding to the finger ridges. "But there's older sign where they went up that way, but there were more that went up than came down. I'm guessing, this was the bunch we saw earlier, but the others might have gone down another trail, maybe to go toward the other stations, thataway," nodding downstream of the Platte.

He stood, looking around, then nodded to the west up the draw that held the river, "Let's go upstream there a ways, then go up top, see if we can find their trail or even their camp. I don't want to use the same trail, give ourselves away." He swung back aboard Blue and reined around to start on the two-track trail, or the rough wagon road that had probably only been used by prospectors and the only wagons being those carrying their prospecting gear.

It was soon obvious the mountains pushed in on the river and there would be few if any side gulches that would serve their purpose. Reuben pointed to the grassy flat beside the narrow river, "Let's stop there and have some coffee, then we'll take this gulch here," pointing to his right, "and go up top."

"I'm all for that. Breakfast wasn't too pleasing this morning. How 'bout some biscuits and gravy?"

Reuben smiled, "You don't need to ask me twice about that!" as he stepped down and took the horses and mule to water.

"I thought we was goin' back to camp! Where we goin' now?" whined Harvey, a man that thought more of his need for food and coffee than most anything else.

"I told John we'd try to meet them at Azel Slaght's Ranch," answered Jim Reynolds, shaking his head in frustration at his brother-in-law who always seemed to fail to see the bigger picture of their venture.

"How'd you know him?" asked Harvey.

"When we were here before, there were several members of the Knights of the Golden Circle that got together, wanting to start recruiting for the south, even before the war. We met him and a few others down in Fairplay," explained Jim, "That's where we met most of the others that have helped us, Guiraud, Bradley, Burr and Jerome in Cañon City, and others."

"They still recruitin'?" asked Harvey, curious about others that were southern sympathizers but never got involved in the fighting.

"Prob'ly not. I reckon they did all they could and like most, prob'ly got discouraged and turned to their own needs."

The men rode in silence for the rest of the way, when they stopped to give the horses a drink and to stretch their legs, Jim explained they would stop at Slaght's for a meal, adding that Azel's wife was an exceptional cook and always enjoyed company. The men were happy to hear that, especially Harvey who's oft used expression was, "I'm so hungry my stomach thinks muh throat's been cut!" Yet several others were feeling that way as the sun had passed its zenith and even though they ate at the Kenosha house, they were looking forward to another meal. It wasn't often they could have two good woman-cooked meals in the same day.

Addison Stowe and Owen Singletary were riding side by side behind Jim and Harvey and had heard the conversation and Owen asked Addison, speaking somewhat quietly, "What's that Knights thing they was talkin' about?"

"You don't know about the Knights of the Golden Circle?" asked Addison, somewhat surprised.

"No, I wouldn't be askin' if I did!" replied Owen. He was the youngest of the bunch and had little experience in the world before leaving the farm to join up with the South.

Addison looked around as if to see if anyone was listening, then leaned closer to the younger man, "It's a secret bunch that's supportin' the South, recruitin' so'jers, givin' money, stuff like that. Most of 'em is in the North and workin' for the South. They got secret signs, passwords, an' all that stuff."

"Are you one?" asked Owen.

"Nah, never had the chance to join 'em, an' now that we're doin' what we're doin', don't see the need."

"Whaddya mean, what we're doin'?" asked Owen.

"You know, desertin' the confederacy, taking the gold for ourselves, you know."

"We're desertin'?" asked Owen, frowning and looking at the others.

Addison shook his head, frowning and looking at the young man, "Yeah," dragging out the word to emphasize the expression, "We done deserted when we started robbin' the stage stations and keepin' the money for our own selves."

"I didn't get no money, did'chu?"

"Jim said he'd divide it up when we get back to camp. Don't worry!" exclaimed Addison, putting some space between the two to end the conversation.

The valley had opened up as the foothills pushed back away from the river bottom. With cottonwoods, alders, and willows hugging the riverbanks, grassy flats had a few cattle from Slaght's ranch that were grazing beside mule deer. As they neared the ranch, two big freight wagons took up most of the road. Jim looked back at the men, "Get ready, we might take these wagons, but don't get antsy!" He turned back to face the oncoming wagons and as the freighters approached a ruddy faced Dutchman made a quick wave and dropped his fist to his chest as if beating his chest. Jim smiled, nodded, made the same sign and greeted the men, "Howdy fellas! Goin' far?" he asked, leaning his hands on his pommel.

"Goin' South!" declared the Dutchman, "Got some cargo for the men on Georgia Gulch. How 'boutchu?"

Jim knew Georgia Gulch was so-called because most of the men prospecting there were from Georgia and good Southerners, it was even known as a hotbed for the Knights of the Golden Circle. "Oh, just lookin' around a mite, seein' if we can find any men that want to join up with us!"

The Dutchman lifted his head in an exaggerated nod, grinned, "Good luck!" he said as he slapped reins to the mules to resume his journey. The men reined their horses to the side, allowing the wagons to pass unhindered.

When they started on their way again, Owen looked at Addison, "How's come we didn't take them wagons?"

"Didn't you see the sign?"

"What sign?"

Addison shook his head, wondering about the smarts of the boy, "That's what we was just talkin' 'bout. Those men are part of the Knights, Jim recognized the sign and did the same. Those fellas are for the South!"

"Oh," mumbled Owen, not certain he fully understood.

Jim led the small party down the wagon road to Slaght's ranch house and was greeted by a balding, pot-bellied man that stood on his porch, stretching his galluses as he hollered at the men, "Well, lookee here! If it ain't Jim Reynolds, right'chere in my front yard! I say, boy, you're beginnin' to make a name for yourself!" He chuckled, motioned to him and the others, "Come on, get down, Ma's got the kettle on and there's enough for you and a whole bunch more!"

Jim chuckled, "Good, cuz we're s'posed to meet muh brother and his men here. You seen him?"

"Did. Early this mornin'! But he an' them others headed thataway," pointing downstream toward Bailey's Ranch, "but hinted he might be back," chuckled the rancher, motioning the men into the house.

Mrs. Slaght set a good table. The big pot held elk stew with potatoes, carrots, onions, and more. Her biscuits were big, fluffy, and tasty, and the men made short work of their portions, washing it all down with coffee black and thick enough to float a rock. They pushed away from the table and started for the door just as they heard other riders approaching. The rancher was quick to go to the porch to see who was coming, recognized John Reynolds and his men and greeted them, "You fellas almost didn't get here soon 'nuff. These others almost licked the pot clean!" as he motioned them into the house.

———

"SO, HOW'D YA DO?" ASKED JIM, LOOKING AT HIS BROTHER as they walked to the barn, seeking some time alone.

"Waste o' time. Bailey's, Junction, none of 'em had anything to speak of, oh, I s'pose we coulda taken a few guns, maybe a couple horses, but wasn't worth the trouble. Even the Toll Gate, they only had three dollars and that was from the Dutchman with the freighters," he paused, kicking at some rocks, looked at his brother, "How'd you do?"

Jim chuckled, "We took the Kenosha House station. Got a good haul of gold dust from the stage, some from the station and a fist full of money!"

John laughed, slapped his brother on the back and said, "Now, that's what I like to hear!"

"Yeah, but some of the men are complainin' we haven't given 'em any. So, I figger we'll take a pouch or two, split it with 'em and maybe even hide the rest. It's too much to be carryin' around with us and anybody that found it would know we are the ones robbin' the stations!"

John stopped, looked at his brother and began to

grin, "You know what'd be a good place? Remember up above where we camped, there was a couple prospect holes? We could go ahead of the men, say we're scoutin' the trails over the top or somethin', and bury it in one o' those holes. If anybody asks, we'll just tell 'em its for safekeepin' and we'll get it 'fore we leave!"

Jim chuckled, "Now you're thinkin'! We could do that yet today," he glanced at the sun, "I think we can make it back up Geneva gulch 'fore dark and get it done, don't you think so?"

John nodded, grinning, "Ummhumm, we can!"

21 / POSSE

"I'm tellin' ya' sheriff, they's a bunch o' killers! And if'n you don' get 'em, more people's gonna die!" declared Abner Williamson, breathing heavy from his long hard ride south from Kenosha House. He'd stopped every place he could to spread the word about the Confederate rebels and their rampage of carnage and thievery. He had dropped to the ground, bent over with hands on his knees, looking a lot like his lathered horse who stood, head hanging, and front legs splayed apart.

Sheriff Jack Sparks sat in his favorite rocking chair that sat on the boardwalk outside the door of his office, giving him a view up and down Front Street. He came forward, elbows on his knees and glared at Williamson, "I heard tell of some Confederate rebels doin' this sort o' thing, is this the same bunch?"

Williamson dropped his head into the water of the horse trough, came up suddenly, tossing his head back, the hair acting like a whip as it carried water that splashed on the boardwalk making the Sheriff jump back to keep from getting wet. The sheriff glowered at the stage driver and asked again, "I said, is it the same bunch?"

"How'd I know, sheriff? I ain't seen the others, but the way they talked with that Southern drawl, then yeah, I'd say they was Confederate sympathizers," replied Williamson, running his fingers through his wet hair and wiping off his face. "So, what'cha gonna do?"

Sparks shook his head, slowly rose from his chair and looked up and down the street, watching the many busy figures going in and out of the stores and taverns, many holding their purchases of tools and more. He looked back to Williamson, "I dunno! I'm the sheriff here in Fairplay and they ain't done much here'bouts. What'chur talkin' 'bout is clear up north and there's other towns 'tween here an' thar."

"But ain't none o' them got sheriffs or any other real law!" growled Williamson, his frustration showing. He had suspected this response from the sheriff, true to his reputation, but had hoped for more. "How's about gettin' a posse of men from all around, that'd give you authority for the whole park!" suggested Williamson.

The sheriff frowned, looking from the stage driver to the many men in the street and about town. He looked back to Williamson, "Which way'd they go after the robbery?"

"Up Kenosha pass, as far as I could tell. We was all tied up and took us a spell to get loose, but their tracks looked like they went thataway."

"They kill anybody?"

"Nope, but they busted up my stage!"

The sheriff frowned and turned to look directly at the man, "Busted up your stage? Why'd they do that?"

"I dunno, meanness I reckon, but they done a good job. Busted the spokes on the wheels, cut the thoroughbraces, smashed the doors an' more." He shook his head as he remembered the damage to *his* coach.

"Well, mebbe I'll see if anyone's interested in bein' on a posse, see if we can do sumpin' 'bout these devils!" He pulled his britches up, and started off toward the town center, planning on finding his recruits in the taverns and elsewhere.

Williamson hollered after him, "You want me to come along!"

The sheriff paused, turned back to face the man and nodded, giving him the come-on sign. Williamson grinned, slapped the rein of his very tired mount around the hitchrail and started after the sheriff. The two men pushed into the nearest tavern, *The Ace of Spades* and paused to let their eyes become accustomed to the dim light. It was mid-afternoon and the place was already getting crowded, most were lined up at the long bar, but several tables were full with every seat taken. Sparks went to the bar, grabbed an empty mug and banged it on the bar to get some attention. When most turned and the noise abated somewhat, he began, "Men! There's been a bunch of outlaws have been robbin' stages, stations, ranches and more. They done kilt three people that we know of, and prob'ly more. They just hit the Kenosha House and stole the gold some o' you were shippin' out to the banks an' such, likewise at the other stations an' stages. You wrote letters to your families, put some money in 'em, and these fellas, some say they're Confederate renegades, are even tearin' open your mail an' takin' the money you meant for your families." He paused to look at the reaction among the men, all of which was less than positive. One man yelled out, "So, what're ya' gonna do 'bout it Sheriff?"

"That's why I'm here. We're gettin' up a posse and

goin' after 'em. We can't let 'em take ever'thing you been workin' for, now, can we?"

The crowd busted out in shouts of "NO!" and much more. Several men stood, "I'll go on that manhunt!" declared one man who looked more like an out-of-work cowboy than a prospector, but the Sheriff wasn't going to be picky. He nodded to the man, saw three others nod and stand, one asked, "What do we need to bring, Sheriff?"

"Your horse, supplies for, oh, maybe a week, your bedroll and a gun and ammunition!"

"S'alright if'n I ride to Buckskin? I know there'e men there that'd wanna come!"

"Have at it, Ben. But we'll be leavin' in a couple hours, so get a move on!"

The Sheriff and Williamson went to two other taverns and had about the same response. As they were leaving, the Sheriff looked at the stage driver and shook his head, "You know, I didn't think there'd be that many willin' to go. So, I reckon we need to get our horses and gear, and you're gonna need a fresh horse cuz I'm sure yours is done played out!"

———

THE POSSE NUMBERED FIFTEEN PLUS THE SHERIFF WHEN they left Fairplay. With stops at Hamilton, Tarryall City, and the diggings on Michigan Creek and more, they had 22 men in the posse. The sheriff, although not much of a leader, began to fill the bigger boots and take full charge. "Williamson here's gonna be my second in command," he declared as they all mounted back up to start their pursuit. "Now, he," nodding to Williamson, "was at the Kenosha House when they hit there, an' he said the tracks showed they took off up the pass, but I'm thinkin' we split up a little, maybe I'll take a bunch o'er the mountain there by way of Guernsey Creek, cross o'er them ridges and check out the upper ends of Hoosier, North Platte, and maybe even Geneva Gulch, then drop down to the Wagon road and hook up with the rest of you."

"But sheriff, that'll take a while, maybe two, three days!" pleaded Williamson.

"Not if we get a move on, if we play it right, we'll flush 'em out in a day or two and be back home right after!" He turned to Williamson, "If you take the rest of the men, head up Kenosha, and check the lower, oh, maybe, half-mile of each of those gulches and any place on the east or south side that looks like a possibility, then we'll cover that country 'fore long, and if'n either of us finds 'em, we'll send a rider after th'others and we'll hit 'em together. No sense in takin' unnecessary chances."

Abner looked at the sheriff, trying to read his expression and knowing all the time his reputation was one that did everything he could to avoid any fight or conflict of any kind. Ab was trying to guess what kind of game the sheriff was playing and guessed he thought if the rebels had a camp in any of those gulches, it would be in the lower end, making it more likely that Ab and his bunch would make first contact and if there was any fight, it would be over before the sheriff got there. Ab shook his head, looked at the rest of the posse, and swung back aboard his mount, watched the sheriff mount up and look to the others.

"Alright men, this half," motioning with a big overhead motion and holding his arm extended with a flat hand like an axe to divide the posse, "on my right, will come with me. The rest of you will follow Williamson.

I've deputized Ab and the rest of you, so we have all the authority we need. Now, good luck to us all, and don't take any unnecessary chances! Keep your head down!" With another glance to the others, the Sheriff started out to the north while Abner Williamson motioned to the others and started toward Kenosha pass.

————

"Riders comin'," declared Reuben, glancing back to Elly. He was leading the pack mule while she trailed behind, "Come on up here beside me."

She nudged the appaloosa along the edge of the wagon road to pull alongside Reuben. The riders he saw had just cleared a slight bend in the road and were stretched out behind the leaders. Reuben knew at once these were the guerrillas and he slipped his Henry from the scabbard to lay across his pommel, then reached for his Remington pistol to loosen it in the holster. The pistol was out of sight under his jacket, and he glanced to see Elly had followed his example, her Henry across the pommel of her saddle. They kept moving toward the band of rebels, but he quickly looked for any escape. The embankment to his left was steep, rocky, and impossible to take with the horses, but a glance to the right showed the willow lined Platte with thick trees on the far bank. He spoke softly to Elly, "If anything happens, take to the creek and the timber, don't look back for me!"

"You better be right behind me, or I'll be mighty upset with you!" she muttered, trying to keep things light, but knowing this bunch was capable of anything.

The leader reined up, lifted a hand before him to stop Reuben, "Howdy friend!" declared the leader. Although Reuben didn't know one from the other, he guessed this was Jim Reynolds and his brother, John, who rode beside him.

"Howdy!" responded Reuben, nodding and trying to appear friendly.

"Looks like you're expectin' trouble," replied Reynolds, nodding to the rifle.

Reuben chuckled, "Can't never be too careful in wild country."

"You're right about that. I heard there's been some trouble in South Park, you know anything about that?"

"Can't say as I do, haven't spent much time around other folks. Me and the missus are kind of on a honeymoon and stayin' shy of most folks. But we're on our way to Golden City, got some relatives up there we're gonna visit with, then ..." and shrugged to suggest their plans were yet to be determined.

The two leaders smiled and chuckled at the 'honeymoon' and glanced at Elly, looked at the big black dog that stood on the far side of the appaloosa, and noticed she appeared to be embarrassed by dropping her head, shaking it and looking away. The men near the front also heard the comment and snickered at the suggestion, but Jim and John looked to one another and Reuben saw a slight shake of Jim's head before he turned to look back at Reuben. "Well, you two have a good honeymoon and watch out for bandits, there's plenty of 'em around these parts, what with all the gold and such."

Reuben nodded, "Thank you, and you fellas do the same!" With a squeeze of his knees, he started Blue forward, Elly's appaloosa staying alongside, and the rebels tipped their hats to the lady as they passed. They waited till they were well away from the bunch before they turned slightly to look back, but both were relieved to see the entire band had disappeared around the bend.

Reuben exhaled as if he had been holding his breath and visibly relaxed as he glanced to Elly, who had slumped slightly as she shook her head before looking directly at Reuben.

They both laughed, the relief showing in their faces, as Elly said, "I just realized, I didn't have a round in the chamber. If I had to shoot it would've just clicked! Think that woulda scared anybody?"

They both laughed again and continued north, until Elly asked, "How far we goin' since we already know where they are?"

"How 'bout right over there," answered Reuben, pointing to a grassy flat beside the riverbank where the willows were sparse and the water close. "Maybe have us a little bit to eat, some coffee, then we'll decide what's next."

Elly smiled and reined the appaloosa off the road, Bear hot on her heels, as they went down the slight slope to the grass and dropped to the ground, relieved and anxious for some coffee. Reuben grinned as he watched her lay back in the grass, arms wide, and eyes on the clouds. Bear rolled in the grass beside her, as Reuben leaned on his pommel, "I don't know how you do it!"

"Do what?" she asked, unmoving.

"Even all stretched out in the grass, you're still the most beautiful woman I've ever seen!"

She sat up on her elbows, smiling broadly, "You sweet talkin' devil you! Come here!" she said as she curled a finger and smiled coyly.

A rocky escarpment about thirty yards above the road, the cut between the hills that were freckled with spruce, fir, and aspen, and a tall rocky pinnacle, all marked the trail that bent to the north away from the Platte. Geneva Creek was maybe twenty feet at its widest and no more than a foot deep with ice cold and clear runoff water that came from the high mountains. The trail sided the creek that cut through the rocky foothills and towering spruce. Jim and John and pushed a little further ahead of the others and John Reynolds asked his brother, "We gonna stash the take as soon as we get there or wait a spell."

"Right away. It'll be gettin' dark soon and I want to get up there while we can still see," answered Jim.

"What'll we tell the others?"

"Just tell 'em we're gonna stash it all 'fore we hit any more outfits, too much to carry. But to make 'em happy, we'll make a point of leavin' some behind and tell 'em we'll split it up when we get back. We can trust Harvey to keep 'em out of it."

"It'd be easier if we leave the greenbacks and stash the

dust and coins," surmised John, glancing to his brother. The trail into the Geneva Gulch hugged the steep hillside, cutting through the trees and following the cascading creek. They had to wait until the crashing water smoothed out to be able to hear one another and Jim nodded but kept pushing on through the trees. From the main wagon road to the upper end of the trail where they had made camp was a little over four miles, far enough away from the road to be undetected, ample water and graze for the horses, and sufficient cover to make their camp easily defensible.

When they broke into the open, Jim led the band to their camp, reined up and stepped down. The others did the same, some plopping on the ground, others seating themselves on the logs or rocks that made up their camp. "Alright men, you get supper together, lay out your bedrolls and such, get plenty of firewood. We'll be splitting up the money when John and I get back. For right now, we're gonna stash the gold and coin up yonder, away from our camp, just in case somebody comes upon the camp."

"Where ya' gonna put it?" asked Addison.

"Dunno. There's some prospect holes up yonder that might do, but we'll find a nice safe place for it and let you know when we get back. Harvey, you and Addison there, count the greenbacks and when we get back, we'll divide it among us. After we make a few more strikes, maybe some stages or mines over the hill yonder," motioning to the mountains to the north beyond which lay Breckenridge and further to California Gulch, both rich strikes, "and we need to have a good place for our camp and the gold. After that, we'll divide everything and go our separate ways."

The men looked at one another, grinning and slapping one another on the shoulder, laughing and squirming about. Jim added, "Now, go 'head on and get everything set. We'll be back shortly."

While Jim was speaking, John and Harvey had been loading the pack mule with the gold pouches and bags and with a nod, John signaled Jim they were ready. Jim nodded, turned back to his horse and swung aboard. John followed suit and grabbed the lead for the pack mule and the two brothers started across the grassy flat, determined to follow the creek into the upper reaches of the long gulch. At the upper end of the long park formed by the twisting Geneva Creek, three other streams converged with Geneva; Burning Bear, Bruno, and Duck Creeks. The trail stayed on the east bank of Geneva and John pointed up Duck Creek, "How 'bout up there, looks good to me."

Jim reined up, looking up the thickly timbered draw, "Naw, too thick up there. Make it to hard to get in and out in a hurry! Let's go a little further," and nudged his mount to keep moving. To their left, a small, pointed butte rose, thick spruce clinging to its slopes, and to the right of the butte, a small park beckoned. "There, I like the looks of that!" stated Jim, digging heels to his mount to quicken the pace. They moved across the grassy flat toward the distant tree line, and a quick glance over his right shoulder showed Jim a prospect hole, while the grassy flat showed a marsh with cattails and willows around a small pond. He turned back to John, "Wait here, hold the horses and mule, I'm goin' up there!" pointing to the rocky scar that marked the prospect hole.

Throughout gold country, the hillsides were marked with gravel dumps below a prospect hole where would-be gold miners just started digging, hoping to hit the mother lode of gold, but most knew very little about gold and where it was to be found. On rare occasions they would make a strike, dig it out, and if profitable, turn the little hole into a deep underground mine.

Jim pushed his way up a narrow trail, came upon the hole and looked around the valley below, nodded and hollered, "This'll do! Start bringin' up the gold!" and quickly returned to the animals to help his brother. They made short work of burying the gold, needing only to push with their boots the diggings back on the pile of pouches and tossing some bigger stones for added security. The two very tired men returned to their horses, mounted up and looked up at the hole, saw nothing different that would be a giveaway, and reined around to return to camp.

John asked, "How much you think is there?"

"I'm thinkin' somewhere around forty thousand, maybe more."

"That's a tidy sum! We can do a lot with that!"

"Ummhumm," replied Jim. He glanced across the little grassy flat, pointing,

"That looks like it might be a shorter way, c'mon," as he nudged his mount off the trail to cut across toward the smaller creek on the far side.

As they came to the small creek, the willows had given way and a wide swath of water moved slowly over a sandy bottom. Jim said, "Ha! That ain't more'n a couple inches deep!" and nudged his mount forward, but the big black was a little skittish, dropping its head to look at the water, trying to sidestep, but Jim hollered, "C'mon horse! Get across there!" and slapped legs to the ribs of the mount, making him jump ahead. One jump was all he made. All four hooves sunk deep into the sand that now showed a thick black mucky mire. The thin layer of sand had been washed over time to cover a deep black bog that stretched several feet in every direction. Jim was kicking the horse, hollering at it, "C'mon! Move!" as the big horse fought the mire. Yet every move caused them to sink even deeper, the horse now chest deep. Jim had kicked free of the stirrups and had his feet on his pommel, as he twisted around, "John, your rope! Throw me your rope!" he screamed.

John was fidgeting with his rope that hung beside his pommel, strapped tight and seldom used, it was difficult to get free. As he finally brought it up, he tried to swing it overhead, making a loop to toss to his brother, but just got tangled as Jim continued shouting. "Hurry! Can't you see we're sinking!" With another try, John finally got the loop to his brother, who grasped it, and hollered, "Back up! Quick!" As John backed his horse away, Jim hollered again, "Now, get it tight!" and as John nodded, Jim stood in his saddle, jumped as far as he could, and landed in the black mud, starting to sink, "Pull me out! Quick!" John reined his mount around, and with the roped wrapped around the saddle horn, dug heels to his mount and slowly pulled Jim free.

Once on solid ground, Jim turned to look at the black, and coiled the rope and stepped as close to the bog as he dared and tried repeatedly to rope the head of his horse. After four or five tries, he finally landed a loop around the horse's head, pulled it tight and looked back at John. He motioned his brother closer and ordered, "Tie that to your horn and pull him out, just like you did me!" Their repeated efforts proved futile as the big horse fought until he was worn out and gave up, slowly sinking into the black bog.

The mule wasn't too interested in letting Jim ride, always moving away when he tried to mount, frustrating Jim all the more, and when John snugged the mule up beside his horse. With no room for the mule to move, Jim finally did get aboard, but as soon as John and his horse moved away, the mule did his best imitation of an angry grizzly, standing on his hind feet, pawing at the sky. But when he dropped to all fours, he tucked his head between his front feet and stretched out to kick his heels at the nearest clouds and launched Jim over his head and into the rocks at the edge of the trees. Jim screamed, jumped up and started picking cactus spines out of his belly and arms. He slowly walked towards John who was doing all he could to keep from loosing a belly laugh, watching as Jim was picking cactus spines from a massive prickly pear cactus all the while and muttering new names for the mule. The big mule stood, front legs splayed apart and looked at Jim as if he was a gargoyle from hades and seemed to dare him to try to get aboard again.

Jim walked to the side of John and his horse, looked up at his brother and said, "Give me the stirrup." John removed his foot from the stirrup, allowed Jim to use it to mount and swing up behind the cantle of John's saddle, and without a word, John swung down to grab the lead from the mule and started back to camp.

The men were surprised to see the brothers riding double, but when Jim stepped down his expression told them not to ask. He looked around the camp, seeing the expectant faces on the men, then frowned, "Anybody see Bobbitt? He was supposed to get some game and have fresh meat waitin' for us."

The men looked at one another, all shaking their heads until Holloman said, "He was talkin' 'bout desertin', goin' off on his own. Mebbe he did." The others looked back at Jim for his reaction, saw the man shake his head and back up to the fire, hands behind him.

Jim looked at Harvey, motioned him near the fire where Jim stood, his back to the flames, as he tried to dry off and warm up. "What'd you come up with?"

"Little over five thousand," answered Harvey.

Jim nodded, motioned for John to come near, "You and Harvey start dividin' up the greenbacks, and there's two bags of dust back by my saddle bags, you," giving a head nod to John, "start dividin' one of those bags among the men. That'll give each of 'em a little over five hundred. That'll keep 'em goin' if we get split up or until we divide the rest. Every'body feels better with a little money in their pockets!"

23 / SIGHTING

"I don't like the looks of this," declared Reuben, turning around in his saddle, looking up the twisting and narrow gulch that held the Geneva Creek. As Bear returned to their side, Reuben said, "Those hills are too steep, and the gulch is too narrow, if we ran onto those rebels there'd be no escape." He looked at Elly who had also noticed the steep walls of the gulch and the narrow trail that often dipped in and out of the narrow creek just to make it around the next bend.

"It is a little claustrophobic," she replied.

Reuben frowned as he looked back at her, "Claustrophobic? If that ain't a big word for 'scary' I don't know what is, but big or little, let's turn around and get outta here. I got a better idea!" He motioned to Bear and brought him back beside them before he made his move to get out of the narrow gulch.

They had just passed the second gulch that held a dry bed runoff. Reuben used a wide spot where the creek bent away from their side of the gulch and led the mule to ride shy of the willows and point the animals downstream. A quick glance above showed a rocky topped knob that marked the end of a long finger ridge that came from the high-up mountain. Another gulch to the lower side of the rocky knob marked the point in the trail where they could see to the bottom of the gulch and the Platte River Road. They had only come about a half-mile up the gulch before turning back and the open spaces offered relief to the concerned riders.

Once back on the main wagon road, they turned to the west to take another route that would give them the high ground. Reuben remembered an arroyo that lay between the two larger gulches and came from the top of the foothills to drop into the Platte valley wagon road. The arroyo showed no sign of any horses or even game trails, but from what he had seen and remembered, it should give them access to the top. They were nearing the arroyo when they heard horses, many of them, coming toward them. Reuben motioned to Elly, and they reined up to wait for the riders to come near. They were surprised to see about ten men, and by the looks of them most were prospectors.

"Howdy!" declared the man in the lead. With a glance around the roadway and the surrounding hills, he looked back at Reuben, "Goin' to South Park are ya?"

"Somethin' like that. And you?"

"We're a posse out of the park and we're lookin' for a band of outlaws, confederate guerrillas, that been maraudin' the countryside, robbin' stages and stations and such." He looked at Reuben, watching for any reaction, then added, "You seen anybody like that?"

"Now, how would I recognize somebody I never saw before? By the way, are you a sheriff or somethin'?"

"We're a lawfully deputized posse, an' Sheriff Sparks deputized us!" declared Abner, getting some remarks from his men as they nodded their agreement. Ab looked past Reuben, apparently recognizing Elly as a woman and frowned, "But I'm guessin' that since you're travelin' with a woman, you ain't one of 'em."

"No, we're not. But the men you're after left Azel Slaght's ranch and took that road up Geneva Gulch," replied Reuben, leaning on his pommel, grinning.

"Now, how'd you know that?" asked Ab, frowning at the man.

"We've been on their trail for some time now. We're goin' up that draw there," nodding behind the posse, "and see if we can get past them or find their camp without them knowin'." As he spoke, he slipped his badge from his pocket, palmed it, and showed it so only the leader could see it.

Ab glared wide-eyed and started to say something, but Reuben nodded to him, gave a slight shake of his head, and Ab twisted around in his saddle to look at the draw, and back to Reuben, "Keep your eyes open, the Sheriff is comin' from the upper end with his posse, 'bout the same size as this'n." He stood in his stirrups to look down the road, "That Geneva Gulch, if'n I recomember right, it's 'bout a couple miles, right?"

"Ummhumm, and it's narrow. So, you might wanna get into the trees soon as you can!"

"We'll do that. How many of 'em are there?"

"'bout a dozen, but they all look like they might be a little desperate and prone to do just 'bout anything to keep from bein' taken."

"We'll keep that in mind. I don't think you're too smart takin' your woman in there with you, but ..."

Reuben grinned, "She's comin' along to protect me!"

Abner shook his head, grinning, "Well, hopefully we'll hook up with the sheriff 'fore we run into 'em." He nudged his mount forward and motioned for the men to follow. As they passed, they glanced to the big dog yet each nodded or tipped their hats to Elly who smiled in return.

When the last men disappeared around the bend, Reuben grinned at Elly who was giggling and looking at her man, "To protect you, huh?"

"That's right, and you do a good job of it, too!" he answered, nudging his mount off the road to take to the arroyo and find a way to the top.

They kept to the dry sandy bed of the runoff draw, letting the horses pick their footing. Bear bounded up the draw without a look back, having no difficulty and appeared to be enjoying himself. After about two hundred fifty yards and a climb of about four hundred feet, the arroyo forked and offered a saddle that appeared to access the upper flats. Reuben glanced back at Elly, pointed at Bear who stood at the edge of the steeper climb looking down on them. Reuben pointed Blue to the lesser draw and dug heels to make him start the climb. The big roan twisted his head around to look at Reuben as if to question his judgement, but another dig of the heels pushed him to start the climb.

The big roan stretched out, humped up and started up the steep draw. Again, Reuben gave Blue his head, letting him pick his own footing, as the lead from the mule drew taut and Reuben was almost jerked out of the saddle. With a determined tug on the lead, the mule followed but did not fight the trail as much as Blue, easily making the steeper climb. The steep part of the climb was just over a hundred yards but as they neared the top, several dead snags that had been the victim of a blow down or old fire, blocked the way, forcing the animals to jump over one log and circumvent the others. Yet, just as they reached the top of the steep climb, the saddle opened up and offered easy moving. Within just a few moments, the sure-footed appaloosa with Elly aboard, followed the newly made trail of the others and joined Reuben at the beginning of the saddle.

As they broke from the trees, they stopped, surveying the grassy bottomed mesa top that rode the foothills between the deeper gulches. Reuben looked off his left shoulder to see the sun beginning to tuck itself away beyond the western horizon as it started to paint the sky with shades of gold. He looked back at Elly, "It's amazing how God can paint such beauty in the midst of all the terrible things that happen."

"It's because He is a God of grace and forgiveness and always has his arms open for us." She nodded to the sunset, "That's his eternal invitation for us to come to Him."

"Well, if it's alright with you, I'll just wait a bit longer before I accept *that* invitation. I'm lookin' forward to Heaven, but I ain't in no hurry to get there!" He waved to Bear, "Scout, Bear!" motioning him to move across the flat.

It was Reuben's thought that the men would be camped in the upper end of the Geneva Gulch, probably having found a sizeable clearing for their camp and ample water and graze for the horses, plus it would need to be far enough from the main road to not draw attention and allow them to have a cookfire. He knew Bear would scout the area, searching for any sign or scent of others or danger which would include the smell of smoke of a campfire. They pushed their mounts into the flats, following Bear who often stopped to look over his shoulder to be certain they were following. With the sun lowering in the west, they would have about an hour of dusk to travel by, then it would be dependent upon the clear night sky and the size of the moon.

They were in a flat-bottomed high-country valley, what some would call a hanging valley, that was nestled between the timbered hills on either side. On their left the low hills were covered mostly with large stands of aspen, black timbered thickets separating the bigger stands of aspen. On their right, the hills were covered with high-country fir and spruce that showed as black timber in the waning light of dusk. It was about a mile when the valley petered out and Bear took a dim game trail that pointed them north in the general direction Reuben knew they would have to go to hit the upper end of Geneva Gulch.

A short distance farther and they broke into one of the many high-country grassy parks of about twenty acres, yet Bear kept to the east edge as he followed the game trail into the thick timber. Shafts of pale moonlight pierced the canopy of pines, offering patches of light as they pushed through the timber, always going slightly downhill and to the northeast. A short distance brought them to another park, where a small herd of bedded down elk stared as they passed. Bear took to what appeared to be a runoff draw and never slowed his pace. Less than half a mile brought them to another park where Bear paused, head lifted, sniffing the air with something getting his full attention as he turned to cross the park and pad quietly through the tundra growth to approach the edge of the park and stop, staring through the thin trees that lined the north edge of the park and overlooked the valley below.

Reuben and Elly rode up behind Bear and when he turned to look at them, they knew to go no further. They dropped to the ground and in a crouch, went to the side

157

of Bear to see what he was focused upon. Below them at the far edge of a narrow basin, a campfire glimmered in the darkness, shadowy figures around it, some moving about, others seated. "That's them!" declared Reuben, speaking softly, watching and counting the men below.

"You're sure that's not the sheriff and the rest of the posse?" asked Elly.

"Ummhumm," he paused, looking around. "Cuz that's the posse comin' there!" he pointed to the upper end of the valley, a little over a mile, where several shadowy riders had just broken from the timber and could be easily seen in the openness of the valley as they rode in the moonlight. It was a natural thing when riding at night to seek the area where the moon gave a better light, but not the smartest thing for man hunters.

R euben turned to Elly, "Do you think you can get down there and warn the sheriff?"

Elly frowned, looked at the treetops and the lay of the land between her and the posse, "I can try, maybe go down that draw," nodding to a dip at the edge of a finger ridge, "go across the flat and catch them."

"Then get after it, they need to be up in these hills above 'em or someplace high!" he suggested as she swung back aboard the appy. "I'll be down lower on this slope where I can get a good line of fire!" he called after her, still trying to keep his voice low enough not to be heard across the valley. Sound carries in the dark more than most realize and anything out of the ordinary would immediately arouse their suspicion. Many a time Reuben had been camped in the wilderness, quickly becoming accustomed to the normal sounds of the night, birds, smaller animals scrounging for food on the forest floor, the calls of other animals like coyotes, wolves, and others. But whenever anything different occurred, although he would be sound asleep, that difference immediately alerted him and brought him to full awareness. That was his concern for this night and the coming of the posse, especially since they were approaching from two directions and the sounds would be multiplied.

He slipped the Sharps from its scabbard, stuffed several paper cartridges in his possibles bag that hung at his side, and with the horse and mule tethered but within reach of ample graze, he started through the trees to work his way closer. The moon had given enough light to show a steep but timbered ridge that bent back to the west, but dropped into the valley below, its shoulder pushing the creek away from its rocky flank. The top of the ridge held an abundance of dead timber, probably a blow down at some time many years past, but although they offered cover, it would also be a challenge to cross the ridge quietly, picking his steps by moonlight. He had to get closer to be able to make out the individuals and if necessary, pick a target.

When he had first spotted them, they were nothing but shadows, dark figures silhouetted by the campfire, and he was more concerned about the leader, the one some had said was Jim Reynolds, having recognized him from the brothers' previous time in South Park as prospectors and well-known southern sympathizers. He was the one they saw on the road, dark hair, average size, clean shaven, nothing significant about the man who could easily get lost in a crowd. Reuben continued to work his way closer, dropping away from the ridge with the downed timber and working toward what appeared as a rocky promontory that was about three hundred yards from the camp.

Once in position, he picked a big flat-topped boulder for his shooting spot, and climbed atop, rifle slung over his back, and bellied down for his first survey of the camp. The darkness made using his binoculars difficult, but he lifted them in hopes of the campfire offering enough light for him to at least get a good look at the camp. As he watched, two men appeared to be handing out something to each of the men, invoking laughter and hoots and hollers from most. *Must be divvying up the money,* thought Reuben, as he lowered the binoculars and slid the Sharps close.

————

ELLY USED A WHISTLE THAT MIMICKED THE *PEENT* OF THE nighthawk. The sound caused the sheriff to rein up and look to the timber to see Elly come from the trees. She waved her hat high as she dug heels to her mount to quickly cross the flat that was covered with willows, alders, and tall grasses. The sheriff drew his pistol but waited for the newcomer to join them and as she neared, he recognized her, but looked behind her for Reuben. As she came close, Elly pulled up in front of the sheriff, "Reuben sent me to warn you! The rebels are camped in the lower end of this meadow, their horses are between them and you, near the trees on the far side. Reuben said you should take to the trees if you want to get closer. He'll be in the trees above their camp."

"How many are there?" asked the sheriff, noticing the other men had drawn near to hear what Elly reported.

"Looks to be about a dozen. They've got a cookfire goin' so they'll be easy to see. Also, the rest of your posse is coming up from below, they should be getting there pretty soon and if they don't see the fire, they might get ambushed!"

The sheriff was known to take his time, look things over, examine the possibilities, and if the odds were in his favor, he might make a move. But there was little time now to do any of that and he was flustered, looking at the woman and around at the men. One man, Doc Cooper, asked, "What're we gonna do sheriff? We can't just sit here an' let Williamson and the others get ambushed!"

"I know, I know. We'll do as Reuben suggested, let's stay close to the trees, yonder," pointing to the trees that were thick on the slopes of the hills on the south side of the valley.

"But the creek's there!" complained another of the men.

"Yeah, and the noise of the water'll cover any sounds we make!" declared the sheriff, nudging his mount forward to move across the flats and get to the trees. Just inside the tree line, a thin game trail showed itself in the moonlight and beckoned to the men. With the trees for cover, the creek to mask their movements, the men lined out single file behind the Sheriff. Elly had taken to the trail to return to the park above where the horse and mule were tethered. She planned on leaving her appy with the others and with rifle in hand, would search out her man.

As the posse rounded a point of a ridge, the glimmer of the distant fire showed the location of the rebels' camp. The sheriff reined up, called the doc alongside, "There it is, we'll stay in the trees till we get to that last point, then move in on foot. Pass the word back to the others." The doc nodded and moved his horse off the trail and into the trees to await the others and relay the message.

———

JIM REYNOLDS WATCHED AS JOHN AND HARVEY HANDED out the greenbacks and a handful of dust to each of the men. Each man grinned widely, looking at each other and to Jim as he stood, his back to the fire, still trying to dry off the black bog mud and get warm. He nodded to each man, chuckling as they laughed and slapped each other on the shoulders. Suddenly one of the men started singing and the others quickly joined in,

> I wish I was in Dixie,
> Hooray, Hooray!
> In Dixieland I'll take my stand, to live and die
>   in Dixie!
> Away, away, away down South in Dixie!
> Away, away,

But Jim's attention was caught when he saw movement just beyond the ring of firelight and he shouted a warning, "Take arms! They're attacking!" It was a familiar warning to all that had been in actual battle and the men rolled, ran, jumped and grabbed firearms. They quickly took cover behind the scattered rocks and few trees, but the fight had already begun.

When Sheriff Jack Sparks saw the men around the fire, he had ordered his men to try to get as close as possible, using the scattered boulders and trees for cover. But the firelight illumined the face of one of the posse men and the alarm was sounded. At the shout of the leader of the band of rebels, Sheriff Sparks fired his pistol, which was the signal for the posse to open fire, and the scattered men began firing rifles and pistols in a rolling thunder that crashed through the trees and echoed back from the surrounding hills.

REUBEN HAD WATCHED THE APPROACH OF THE POSSE AND had already made ready from his promontory. He moved the rifle from one target to another, not wanting to start shooting if it were possible for the sheriff to take them without a fight, but once the shooting started, Reuben carefully watched each of the rebels, ready to take a shot, if need be, but waiting. After the first volley, the rebels returned fire and the posse men took cover. It's one thing to give chase when you can't see the men, but quite another when they are shooting at you, and the prospectors buried their faces in the dirt and grass, hoping against hope they would be safe.

After the return volley, Reuben heard the leader of the rebels shout to his men, "Take to the trees, save yourselves!"

Some of the men rolled or crawled, refusing to show themselves, all working toward the trees to the far side of their camp. But as Reuben watched, he saw the sheriff rise from behind a boulder and search the camp for any men, looking for the rebels to surrender, but no one showed themselves. Yet one man, hidden by a tall spruce, was taking aim at the sheriff with a rifle. Reuben quickly took aim and dropped the hammer. The big Sharps bucked and spat smoke, prompting Reuben to rise up to see if his aim was true and the targeted man, jerked and fell beside the rock, unmoving. Another man, who appeared to be leader, Jim Reynolds, was covering the escape of his men and was aiming at one of the men in the posse, when Reuben, just finished reloading the Sharps, took a quick aim and fired. His bullet hit the man, but he didn't drop. He grabbed his arm and ducked away from the tree, taking to the darkness to make his escape.

Elly had heard the boom of the Sharps and worked her way through the trees toward Reuben. As she neared, she called out, "Reuben, Reuben, it's me!"

"Come on," he answered, keeping his eyes on the camp. He could make out movement at the horse herd and knew the men were grabbing their horses to make their escape, but the darkness and thick trees would prevent the posse from giving chase. As he watched, he saw the other men of the posse come from the road at a thundering run, probably thinking they were coming to the rescue, but were soon stopped by the uplifted hand of the sheriff. "Hold it! Hold up there Williamson!" He stood in the road and was easily seen by the men who brought their animals to a stop and began peppering the sheriff with questions.

Elly looked at Reuben, "Did you have to shoot?"

"Ummhumm. There were a couple trying to take out the sheriff. I dropped one and wounded the other. I think the wounded one was the leader, Jim Reynolds."

"Did the sheriff and his men get any?"

Reuben chuckled, "Well, near as I can tell, they killed one spruce, two fir trees, and several rocks, but weren't none of 'em Confederates!"

Elly laughed, shaking her head. She looked up at Reuben as he stood, "Are we going to go after them?"

"Prob'ly, but the way they scattered, I think every one of 'em went a different direction. But I'm thinkin' they'll prob'ly head back the way they came. I don't know how well they know this country and men that are running usually go to the familiar. So, maybe after we get a little sleep, we'll go after 'em."

Reuben and Elly rode through the trees to the valley below to meet with the sheriff and see about his plans. When they broke from the trees, the men of the posse were gathered about the campfire, some picking through the leavings of the outlaws, others just warming themselves by the fire. Reuben and Elly rode closer to the fire, calling out before they neared, and were invited to join them. But Reuben and Elly had no plans to stay with the others, especially after what they saw at the edge of the camp. One man that had been killed, had been decapitated, and both frowned and looked away and to the sheriff. Reuben moved Blue closer, "What's with the headless body back there?"

"He was the only one kilt!" laughed the sheriff, "And the doc here," motioning to Doc Cooper, "done cut his head off an put it in a sack. Said he needs it for *Scientific Study!* But I think he's just gonna display it as a trophy!" chuckled the sheriff and the others nearby.

"Do you know who killed him?" asked Reuben.

"Nope! Don't matter nohow, he's dead!" replied the sheriff, who passed a bottle he had been holding to the man beside him and watched as the man tilted the bottle up and took a deep swig.

"What are you gonna do now, sheriff?" asked Reuben, anxious to get away from the men, especially since the liquor had come out.

"Well, since we scattered 'em, I reckon they ain't no threat no more, so we'll just go on back to town in the mornin' and forget about 'em."

Reuben could tell by the manner of the man that he would use any excuse he could to get back to his rocking chair on the boardwalk. Relieved he had not been shot, and that he had not lost any men, he was quite willing to pass the bottle for all to share in the jubilation. Reuben just looked around the bunch, shook his head, and reined Blue away from the fire and with Elly at his side, and the mule eagerly following, Bear took to the trail to lead the way away from the foolishness.

Reuben looked at Elly, "Let's go back the way we came."

"Really? Isn't that kind of a long way around?"

"Maybe not. If I was one of those outlaws, I'd want to go where they didn't expect me and make way toward where I'd want to be, like down south of the park, maybe down by Cañon City." He chuckled as he thought about, "I think the sheriff, if he goes after 'em at all, he'll be goin' toward Denver or Golden City, but I think those fellas will be wantin' to get back to friendly country and that'd be south."

They made camp in the same park where they had previously tethered the horses before the set-to at the rebels' camp. It was high up, wide open but with cover at the edges and they rolled out their blankets under the tall spruce. After digging out a place for their campfire, stacking the dirt high around the edges to prevent it being easily seen, they started the fire and made a quick supper from the supplies carried by the mule. It was a simple supper, cornmeal dodgers, crisp bacon and black coffee, but it did the job and they soon turned in to their blankets, leaving the animals on guard as they were tethered nearby. Bear lay beside Elly and would protect her with his life. They slept soundly but awoke with the rising sun splitting the sky with a long line of grey that shadowed the distant mountains, but it was enough for Reuben to roll out and begin preparing for their hunt.

From the lower end of the small park to the upper end and the trail that would take them higher was no more than a half mile. As they left the little park and took to the aspen and the trail they made the night before, it dropped into the narrow draw that came from the next park higher up, the draw usually carried spring runoff, but the sandy bottom offered good footing for the horses, but Reuben reined up just as they came to the sandy bottom. He looked up and down the draw, dropped to the ground and examined two sets of hoof prints left by horses that were probably ridden by two of the men from the rebels' camp on their escape from the attacking posse. He looked up at Elly who had pushed past the pack mule, "Two of the rebels," he nodded uphill, "looks like they're headin' south!" He chuckled as he shook his head, swung back aboard Blue, "We'll have to keep an eye out. I don't think they'll stop anytime soon, probably want to put as much distance between the posse and themselves, but it's best to be extra careful."

And they did move cautiously, Bear scouting ahead, Reuben and Elly staying close to one another. Yet the tracks before them took the same trail they used to come to Geneva Gulch. Having gone a little bit further to the small park where the elk had been bedded down, Reuben stopped again and looked at the tracks. He shook his head and turned back to Elly, "Two more have joined up," he looked back at the trail, "dunno if there'll be more, but we're on the right trail, sure 'nuff." He swung back aboard Blue and pushed on up the trail that cut through the black timber to the highest park and the way back to the main road.

Once they crested the ridge, dropped into the bigger park he stopped, leaned down to look at the tracks of the four horses, turned to face Elly, "They're cuttin' straight across there, prob'ly gonna either drop in the next gulch, maybe go down to the main road, but unless they can make it 'fore full daylight," he glanced at the rising sun that warmed their back, "they might stay in the trees, but we'll go to the main road, maybe make better time."

Within a short distance, they crossed the old trail used by the rebels when they first went to Geneva Gulch, moving cross country. Reuben pointed Blue down that trail to take them back to the main road. Long shadows stretched across the road, dust hung in the air from either freighters, a stage, or riders. But they had crossed no fresh tracks and with a nod, Reuben started up the road, watching the high banks that lay in the shadows, his hand on his pistol, thumb on the hammer. When they came to the point where Kenosha Creek merged with the Platte, the trail they had used before was now thick with fresh tracks. He looked back to his right, saw where the five horses of the rebels had crossed the road and taken to the bench of the Kenosha.

Reuben looked at Elly, she nodded, and he turned off the road to cross the shallow creek, push through the willows and climb the bank to the bench. As they followed the tracks, the bench made a dog-leg bend to the east and the tracks stayed on the bench. Reuben saw the faint sign of where he and Elly had come from their camp that overlooked the wagon road just a couple days past, but he pushed on to follow the others. It was just over three miles to the end of the bench, "They're still headin' to the east, if they were going down into the park, they would've taken that notch we just passed that would take them down to the ranch of the Matthews."

"I'm glad they didn't go there, I don't think the Matthews would survive a visit from these butchers!" growled Elly, prompting Reuben to look at his woman with a question on his face, "Well, they are! How many have they killed? Four or more that we know of, and probably a lot more. We have to stop them!" she stated as she slapped legs to the Appy and took the lead with only a glance over her shoulder at a flabbergasted Reuben.

"Whoa! Remind me to not get you mad at me!" he mumbled as he nudged Blue to follow.

Elly stayed close on the trail with Bear in the lead and often looking over his shoulder to be certain they were following. At the end of the bench, the trail of the rebels crossed a bit of a saddle on a dim game trail that dropped on the south side and started through a scattered bunch of aspen. "Looks like these trees have had a hard time!" declared Elly, looking back at Reuben and nodding toward the many standing dead snags and the grey logs that had shed their white bark and now lay scattered like the remnants of some great battle against the elements. The trail was hard packed and rocky as it moved through the quakies, the few that still clung to their leaves waved and rattled at the passersby.

When they broke from the aspen, the tracks of the rebels followed the draw that was thick with willow and alders, but with a game trail that sided the thickets. "Hey, hold up a minute," called Reuben, pushing Blue to come alongside Elly's appy.

"What?" she asked, showing her frustration. Reuben thought she must be almighty anxious to catch up to those killers.

"I'm thinkin' they'll be followin' the trail that sides the hills yonder and takes 'em to the south end of the park. They'll want to be near cover, just in case they're spotted, and there's some ranches thataway they could get some supplies or at least a meal."

Elly looked down the draw and saw the timber covered hills that rose on the east edge of South Park, then looked back at Reuben. "So, what do you want to do?"

"I think we need to start back across the valley, see if we can cut sign from any of the others headin' south, cuz I'm pretty sure they had a plan that they would all meet somewhere south, maybe down towards Cañon City. And, we could use some fresh supplies and maybe we can talk to the sheriff and see what he has planned."

"He's already proved to be worthless, so why talk to him?" she asked, leaning forward on her pommel. "Didn't he have a chance to take 'em all and they all got away, all except the one you shot?"

"Yeah, but there's also the Third Colorado Cavalry that has some troops or volunteers at least, and they might be wanting to join in the chase."

"Alright. If that's what you want, but mark my words, I'm bettin' ain't none of 'em in a hurry to get into a fight with the rebels!" she responded, kicking her horse to continue on the trail. When they came to the end of the long draw, it was evident that the previous riders had cut across the two-track wagon road and took to the edge of the trees, their tracks pointing south. Elly stopped, motioned Reuben forward, "Alright. You take the lead," she declared, motioning him to move past her, and with a smile at his humbled wife, he nudged Blue forward and pointed him across the upper end of the park.

As they rode into the edge of Fairplay, they spotted Sheriff Jack Sparks leaning back against the side of his office, his rocking chair propped up as he whittled on a stick. He looked up as Reuben and Elly rode past, nodded, and watched as they made their way to *Granny's café*. As they tethered their animals at the hitchrail, the sheriff walked up on the boardwalk and asked, "Find 'em?"

"Workin' on it," replied Reuben. "So, you buyin' our lunch?" he asked, grinning at the sheriff. The sheriff shook his head, tossed his whittled stick beside the water trough and motioned for them to follow him into the café. Elly gave Reuben a disgusted look, but he just nodded, grinning and whispered, "At least we get a free lunch!"

"Ain't no such thing, don'tcha know?" she answered as she accepted his hand to help her up on the boardwalk.

Reuben seated Elly, pulled out a chair for himself and as the sheriff was seated, the waitress came for their order. As she poured the coffee she said, "Special for the day, bear stew with new potatoes and carrots."

The sheriff nodded, "That'll be fine Maddy," and looked to Elly and Reuben for their order. Reuben looked at Elly who had scrunched up her nose at the 'bear stew' and chuckled, "We're not *that* hungry, how 'bout some o' that fresh apple pie?"

"I don't know how fresh you'd call dried apples, but I'll bring you some." She glanced to Elly, "You too, ma'am?"

"I'll try the pie, but keep the coffee coming, please," she responded, slowly shaking her head.

As the waitress returned to the kitchen, Reuben looked at the sheriff, "So, any plans?" he did not elaborate, assuming the sheriff knew he was referring to the Reynolds gang.

"Nary a one! I figger them fellas are long gone and

are somebody else's concern. We done chased 'em plum outta the country!"

Reuben let a slow grin split his face as he looked up at the sheriff, "You're prob'ly right sheriff, they are purt'near plum outta the country. Trouble is they came right through your territory to do it! They fled south from Geneva Gulch, and are prob'ly even now, oh, somewhere in the south end of the park."

The sheriff frowned, scowling at Reuben, "How's come you know that?"

"We trailed 'em. They cut across country from Geneva Gulch, came across the trail there, up over the hills and cut across the wagon road where Kenosha Creek meets the Platte."

The sheriff dropped his head, mumbling as he fidgeted in his seat. "I'll swear, I was hopin' they was plum gone!" He paused, furrowed his brow and relaxed with a slight grin, "But, if they're at the south end and movin' south, they ain't my concern!"

Reuben shook his head and looked up as a uniformed man approached the table. The sheriff saw Reuben's expression and turned in his chair to see Lieutenant Shoop of Company A, 3rd Colorado Cavalry step to his side. He nodded to Reuben, tipped his hat to Elly and scowled at the sheriff, "Sparks! What's this I hear about you'n that bunch of Confederates?"

The sheriff responded, "Oh, don't get your suspenders in a knot Cap'n. Have a seat and get a cup o' coffee and we'll talk about it."

The captain looked again at the strangers, back to the sheriff, "This is a legal matter, sheriff."

The sheriff glanced from the captain to Reuben and back as he grinned, "Oh, I know Captain, let me introduce you to Deputy Marshal Grundy and Deputy Marshal Grundy," nodding to Reuben and Elly in turn.

The captain frowned, looking from Reuben to Elly and back again, "I don't understand ..." as he took a seat, still looking at the couple.

Elly smiled and explained, "Nothing to understand Captain. Both my husband and I are

Deputy Marshals, originally appointed by Governor Gilpin, and reaffirmed by Governor Evans."

The captain frowned, turned his attention back to the sheriff, "So, what happened?"

The sheriff drew a deep breath and started relating the events of the previous two days and nights, ending with the escape of the outlaws.

The captain shook his head, "So, you just let 'em go?"

"Wal, we thought they'd done gone north and that was outta my jurisdiction, so we came on back."

"Wait a minute, you said you thought they had, but now?"

"Wal, the marshal here says they tracked 'em cross country and they cut back south, came across the park and are now headed in the direction of Cañon City, the way they come into the park in the first place."

"And what are you going to do?" asked the irritated captain.

"Wal, I've been givin' it a lotta thought, and near as I can figger, by the time I'd get a posse together and take off after 'em, they'd be long gone anyway, so why bother? After all, they ain't my headache no more."

The captain abruptly stood, mumbling something about *lazy, no-good sheriff* and stormed out of the café. He had just passed through the doorway when the waitress brought their order and the three, after a brief prayer of thanks, began to make the food disappear. Once finished, Reuben looked at the sheriff, "We need to get a few supplies and we'll be on our way sheriff." He stood, gave Elly a hand up, and turned back to shake hands with the sheriff. "We might not see you again sheriff, so good luck with the job!"

The sheriff nodded, accepted Reuben's offered hand and replied, "And you be careful as you go after them rebels," he looked directly at Reuben, frowned, "you *are* going after 'em ain'tcha?"

Reuben grinned, "Yes, sheriff. We'll be going after them." And turned away to exit the café. The Platte City Mercantile was across Front Street from the café and they walked across the street to enter the store that was the hub of most activity in the town. Their needs were few and the order quickly filled, making a couple of bundles easily handled by Reuben. Elly looked around for the young man, Johnathan, who had shown an interest in Estrella, but he was nowhere to be seen. They had thought to visit with Estrella, the young woman who had been trusted to their care, while they were here, but she was busy with the Reverend Dyer and had gone to Buckskin to help in setting up for a meeting.

With one last look around, Elly shrugged and started for the door. She opened the door for the package laden Reuben and they crossed to the horses and pack mule to stash the goods in the panniers. Once everything was fastened down, they mounted up and started from the town.

With just a glance back, Elly said, "I don't know how that man can sleep at night! With a total lack of concern for the responsibilities of his job and the safety of the people, it's a wonder he's still in office!"

Reuben chuckled, "Elly, you know as well as I do that

if every public official that was worthless at their jobs were suddenly canned, there wouldn't be any politicians, lawyers, sheriffs, and more. There's just something about the supposed security of a public official that seems to render them without conscience and ambition, comfortable in the confines of their office and secure in their position. I'm of the belief that every public official should only serve one term of no more than four years, then make 'em get a real job. Maybe then they'd appreciate the privilege of representing the people that elected them!"

"Oh, sorry. I didn't mean to get you started on your pet peeve!" she giggled, "But you know I agree with you, don't you?"

Reuben laughed, "You're probably the only one that does!"

"So, what's the plan?" asked Elly, riding side by side with Reuben, the big black dog trotting alongside her appaloosa.

"I'm still thinkin' they're headin' south, and if they stop anywhere in particular, it'll be at that same ranch where they stopped on the way into the park. What was the name of it ...?" he frowned as he tried to remember.

"Nineteen Mile ranch, remember, I thought we oughta stop and ask the folks about the rebels, and you wanted to keep going?"

"Yeah, yeah. I remember on the sign it had the names Byers and Young, maybe that's where they'll be hiding out."

"So, does that mean that's where we're headin'?" asked Elly.

"Ummhumm," answered Reuben, obviously thinking about any other possibilities.

He knew there were two roads that came into the

park from the south. One that intersected with the road over Ute pass that came from Colorado City, and the other they had traveled along Currant Creek that joined the stage road at the Hartsel ranch. With a glance to the sky and the position of the sun, "I reckon we'll make it past the Hartsel ranch 'fore we need to camp, maybe at the same place we camped comin' up, there by Thirty-Nine-mile Mountain."

"Suits me, I've had enough of people anyway and a little time by ourselves would be just fine with me!" she declared, smiling at her man. "You gonna get us some fresh meat for supper?"

"Depends on what we see. I'd like to get us some buffalo, it's mighty good eatin', and there was sign in the south end of the park. Maybe we'll get lucky."

"Uh, don't the natives usually follow the herds for their summer hunt?" asked Elly, shading her eyes as she looked to the south.

Reuben saw her expression and heard the hesitation in her remark which prompted him to rein up and reach back for the binoculars in his saddle bags. He slipped them out of the case and brought them to his eyes, looking at a dim dust cloud and spotted the brown mass that was unmistakably buffalo. He moved the binoculars to the far end of the herd and saw nothing but dust, but he also knew Elly was right in what she said about the natives.

"Isn't this the area that Kaniache's people come on their summer hunt?"

"Uh, I think so, but I'm not real sure about that. I know that sometimes the Jicarilla come this far, but I'm not too sure about the Ute," answered Reuben.

"Well, I'm thinkin' we better find us a camp and make

sure we're not out in the open," suggested Elly, looking back at Reuben who lowered his binoculars to look at his woman.

"I think you're right."

27 / UTE

It was not a big herd, but large enough for a good hunt. The encampment of the natives, seen by Reuben through his binoculars, was in the basin between two long finger ridges that came from the west end of the mountain, extending to the north. The big yet lone timber covered mountain that sat like a black island in the middle of the prairie grass of the low end of South Park, a landmark known by anyone in South Park. This was a herd comprised of break-away bands from the larger herds that migrated from the south into the prairie grass land of Kansas Territory and what had recently been marked off as Colorado Territory. The surrounding terrain of South Park was prohibitive to the usual migrations that kept to the flat lands, but many were drawn by the greenery of the foothills and enticed by the fertile plains of the high country. The herd would number in the hundreds, but not nearly the size of the herds of thousands that were known to be found in the plains east of the Rockies.

Reuben and Elly took to the high-up flanks of a solitary butte that sat in the shadow of Thirty-Nine-mile Mountain, choosing a campsite within the tree line of the fluttering quakies. As they came from the rough wagon road that crested Currant Creek Pass, they crossed the trail of five riders that Reuben quickly recognized as the trail of the five men they followed through the Kenosha Creek bench. He pointed it out to Elly, "That's the same bunch we been followin' and they're still headin' south toward that ranch they stopped at before." He frowned as he reined up and looked at the sign, "One thing's confusin' though. We crossed the sign of three others that looked like they were from the same bunch, remember in the flats where we crossed Tarryall Creek? But we haven't crossed them here, at least not yet."

"Maybe they went toward Colorado City or around the bigger mountain yonder," nodding toward the long timbered ridge.

"Well, some of the buffalo came through here," pointing to the churned-up soil on the low flanks of the big ridge, "but most of 'em came around the far side. And if those other fellas went thataway, there's no tellin' where they went from there, not with the herd coverin' their tracks," resolved Reuben.

"One problem at a time. Right now, we might have a problem with the Ute, and if not, we can still go after those five," pointing to the tracks before them, "and worry about the others later."

"Yeah, you're right. Let's get us a good camp," and with a nod to the lowering sun, "and maybe get us some fresh meat."

They quickly made camp below a slight saddle that lay between the crest of the rocky butte and the lower rocky-top knob to its south. The shoulder of the butte offered ample cover from the elements and a little spring with a small pool not much bigger than a saddle seat, but enough for the horses and when they had their fill, a little time allowed it to slowly refill to provide water for their coffee and more. The juniper and aspen would dissipate any smoke from their cookfire, and the fescue and gramma grasses made for good graze and good bedding.

With a look at the sun as it was cradled in the western mountains, Reuben said, "I think a buffalo hunt is off for now, if we got one, which I'm sure will happen, we'll be butcherin' after dark and fightin' wolves and coyotes for every piece of meat! And that's not allowin' for any of Kaniache's hunting parties!"

"Good thinking," answered Elly, "besides, we've got enough for supper, and we can even manage breakfast. If we take one early in the morning, we'll get our cuts and get outta here before we get into trouble!"

"I like your way of thinking!" grinned Reuben, pulling her close for an embrace.

———

THE FIRST LIGHT OF MORNING SAW REUBEN ATOP THE partially bald knob of the high butte that offered a panoramic view of the south end of the Park and the flanks of the timbered crest of Thirty-Nine-mile Mountain. With binoculars at his eyes, he scanned the scattered herd of buffalo, and searched for sign that would confirm his suspicion as to the location of the Ute encampment. Currant Creek Pass was at his back and the wide valley below and the high flanks of the big mountain held the entire herd of buffalo. They had moved south into the higher and greener hillside and were now rising and beginning to graze. From his promontory to the tree line high up on the ridge was about a mile and a half. With the basin stretching about five miles back to the southeast, and north into the wide-open South Park, the buffalo would probably stay the entire summer here.

Movement to his left and north caught his attention and he swung the binoculars to see the hunting party of the Mouache Ute moving around the north end of the herd, the faint light of early morning showing them as little more than shadows. It did not require much imagination to know they were planning on flanking the herd by moving around the bigger buttes to Reuben's left or north and coming at the herd just below his butte. Their timing would be right for them to approach from the long shadow of the butte and using the long dry gulch for cover. Reuben glanced back at the trees around their campsite and saw a thin wisp of smoke rising through the trees and chose to return to the side of his woman. Bear had stayed with Elly, but Reuben had a bit of an uncomfortable sensation that prompted the hair on his neck to rise and he quickly cased the binoculars and with rifle in hand, quickly slid, and ran back down the steep hillside to the camp.

Bear was lying beside Elly as she tended the cookfire and the makings of their early breakfast, neither showing concern or alarm but focused on their task. Reuben scanned the trees and trail below the camp, looking through the scattered aspen and slowly walked into the open, rifle held at the ready. Elly glanced up, saw the concern on his face and tensed up and quietly asked, "What's wrong?"

"Dunno, got a feelin'. The Ute are coming around the

far point. I thought they'd be cutting between this butte and the far knob, but ..." his sentence hung in the air as Bear suddenly came to his feet, a low growl coming from deep in his chest as he looked to the bald slope below the aspen. Riders had spread out and were coming near, the hunting party of the Ute.

Reuben motioned to Elly, spoke softly, "Keep your rifle handy, your pistol out of sight, and don't look alarmed." He stepped to the side of Bear, dropped to one knee and rubbed the big dog on the scruff of his neck, "Easy boy, easy. Just protect Elly." He stood, backed away from the fire and went to a big flat rock that sat near their blankets. The horses were tethered in the trees and out of the way. Reuben lay his rifle across his lap, the hammer cocked, and leaned forward, elbows on knees, to wait for the approach of the Ute.

Five warriors had dropped to the ground, spread out and approached through the trees, weapons at the ready. Reuben watched as they neared, waiting for their close approach. One man, impressive in his size, manner, and appearance stepped forward. With long braids that hung over his shoulders, a wide silver band on one upper arm, hair-pipe bone breast plate, fringed leggings and a beaded breechcloth, with three feathers in a top knot fluttering at the back of his head, his glowering expression showing a mixture of hate, determination, and surprise, he growled, "Why are you here?"

Reuben chuckled, slowly stood and dropped his rifle to his side, "Is this how the Kaniache, the great war chief of the Mouache Ute greets his friends?" stepping toward the intruder. He extended his hand and said, "I am Reuben, and this is Elly, your neighbors in the valley of the Sangre de Cristos."

The war chief's stoic expression did not change as he

glanced down at the extended hand. He held his Spring-field rifle across his chest as he glowered at the white man, and with a grunt gave a slight nod, "I know who you are. Why are you here?"

Reuben motioned to a grey barkless log that lay about eight feet away from the fire, and Kaniache, with a glance to the big dog that stood beside the woman, watching his every move, walked to the log and as Reuben returned to his seat on the nearby rock, he answered, "We have been after some outlaws that have been killin' some folks in the South Park area, they were headin' south when we saw the herd and thought a buffalo steak would taste mighty good. Would it be alright for me to join your hunt? We don't need a whole buffalo, too much meat for just us, but I could take three or four for your people."

The chief looked from Reuben to Elly, nodded to the coffee, "You have coffee?"

Elly chuckled, grabbed another cup and poured their visitor a cup and as she handed it to him, she explained, "We don't have enough cups for the rest of your men."

Kaniache grinned, shrugged, and accepted the offered cup. A quick sip of the boiling hot brew did not change the man's expression as he looked up to Reuben. With a glance to the rifle that lay across the white man's lap, "You are good with that?" nodding to the rifle.

"Ummhumm, good enough."

"These men you are chasing, this many?" holding up one hand, all fingers extended. "One injured, bleeding arm?"

"That's right."

"They passed through yesterday, dusk, following that road," pointing to the road below the camp that followed Currant Creek south.

"There were three others, did you see them?"

He nodded, finished his coffee and said, "They went through there, before the buffalo, to the far end of the long ridge where our village is camped." He stood, motioned to him, "Let's hunt."

Kaniache dispatched his hunters to their previously assigned positions to begin the hunt. He stayed behind to explain the tactics to Reuben to give him the choice of his shooting position. Kaniache bent down to draw in the dirt as he explained, "At my signal, the first group will come from the trees here," pointing to the tree line just below the crest of the high timbered ridge known and Thirty-Nine-Mile Mountain. "That will be the signal for this group," pointing to the south end of the wide sloping plain that fell from the ridge, "to begin their chase. They will start the herd this direction," drawing a line from the south end of the sloping plain to the wide-open northern end. "There are hunters with rifles here," jabbing at a point on the east flank of the high butte north of their campsite on the small knob, "and here," driving the stick into the dirt at a drop-off at the north flank of the big ridge that held an island of timber that lay on the north slope of that drop-off.

Reuben had carefully watched Kaniache's explanation of the tactics of the hunt, recognized the knob with their camp which afforded him a position that over-

looked the low swale. That would probably be the
chosen route of escape for the herd and allow him an
opportunity for several shots at the passing buffalo. "I
will be here," he responded, pointing with the toe of his
moccasin. "How many should I try to take?"

"We have several lodges without good hunters. Whatever you take will be used," explained Kaniache, rising
and swinging aboard his mount. With a somber nod, he
reined around and took off after his hunters. It would be
up to him to give the signal to start the hunt. Reuben
glanced at the pale pink shades of the underbellies of
clouds that lay low in the sky and the increasing light of
the rising sun, still hidden behind the long ridge, and
muttered a simple prayer for safety for the hunters and
success for the hunt. He quickly explained the plans to
Elly, "But if you stay here in the camp, you'll be safe," he
assured her as he held her shoulders with his big hands.

She smiled up at him, "And just what is there about
me that makes you think I am one to stay behind where
it's safe?"

He frowned, shook his head and let a slow smile split
his face, "Alright, c'mon. We're walkin' down to that
rocky shoulder yonder," nodding with his head to the
east edge of the low butte.

She grabbed her Henry, "C'mon Bear," and trotted to
catch up to her man. They had no sooner dropped to the
rocky promontory than the screams and shouts of the
first band of hunters bounced off the buttes and echoed
across the long sloping flanks. A quick glance to the herd
showed heads lifted, the herd bulls turning to face the
possible threat. The mounted hunters swarmed from the
trees, charging down the slope toward the unmoving
herd. But when the second group to the south rose up,
shouting and screaming, some waving and snapping

blankets, the herd lifted as one and turned to flee the surprising threat.

The mass of brown began to move as if joined together, bulls and mature cows taking the lead and flanks to protect the calves and mothers. Massive heads swinging side to side, beards dragging in the grasses, dust beginning to rise in a massive cloud as the hundreds of animals began their flight. The swath of deep brown moved like a blanket, swarming and sliding over the contours of the slope, slipping into the lower edges and following the herd leaders as they charged into the wide runoff draw. Yet the banks of the draw were trampled by the massive beasts, some weighing well over a ton and driving their big hooves into the loose soil, churning the ground as they passed.

The mounted hunters, most using bows and lances, shouted and screamed war cries as they charged the herd, reining their mounts with leg pressure. The proven horses, chosen by riders for this very purpose, matched their gaits to that of the rumbling herd, moving along-side the targeted animals, giving their riders the closest possible advantage to drive their lances deep or send a flint-tipped arrow into the vital parts. Some of the targeted animals did nose dives, driving their massive head into the dirt and flipping over, the thick wool capes and crowns filled with dust and dirt, splashing dust clouds as they impacted the earth. Others staggered, falling on their bellies with noses plowing a furrow better than a farmer's plow.

As the herd neared the low butte, Reuben watched through squinted eyes, searching for targets that were young bulls or cows without calves. His first chosen target, a young bull that lumbered near, keeping to the edge of the herd, until the Sharps roared, the sound muffled by the rumbling thunder of the stampeding herd, and sent the big lead slug deep into the lower chest of the bull, causing him to stumble, bellow, fall to his side and slide to a stop. Reuben had already dropped the breech and jammed another paper cartridge into the chamber, lifting the lever to close the breech and cut the paper holding the powder. Placing another cap on the nipple, he brought the hammer to full cock and with his sight picture on another bull, the Sharps bucked again, and another beast fell.

The repeated blasts of the big Sharps caused the herd to move further away from the butte, but before the entire herd passed and the last of the mounted hunters in their chase were shrouded in the cloud of dust, Reuben had dropped four animals, three bulls and one lone cow. He stood, watching the herd continue to the north, fleeing into the open end of South Park, the brown blanket moving over the terrain like a floating shroud that hugged the contours of the land. He frowned, squinting, then shaded his eyes as the sun crested the long ridge, and muttered, "Hope they didn't get run over!"

Elly looked at him, then turned to look in the direction he was gazing. "Who?"

"Kaniache said there would be a group of hunters with rifles there," he pointed to the north end of the killing fields, "Just below that little ridge. The far side has a thick batch of timber, but if the herd didn't split and go around ..." he left the thought hanging for a moment, then continued, "Looks like that herd went right over there." He continued to look as the dust cloud cleared, saw the churned up soil where the big herd had passed and it appeared the herd *had* charged right through that patch of timber. He shook his head, "Let's get your kit, go see if they need some help." He motioned for Elly to lead the way back up through the trees to their camp.

What had been a cluster of juniper and piñon, rocks and oak brush, that was about sixty yards wide and thirty yards deep that lay on the north edge of the drop off of the low ridge, was now a scattering of scraggly juniper and piñon trunks. The herd had crashed through the patch, crushing almost everything in its path. Injured hunters were scattered about, some having taken shelter behind downed trees or clusters of rocks, others crushed among the debris. Two were obviously dead, trampled beyond recognition. Five others were sitting against the rocks and trees, holding themselves and looking about with wide, terrified eyes. Reuben and Elly were the first to come to their sides and quickly began ministering to their needs, bandaging open wounds, cleaning injuries where possible, binding up broken limbs. They were soon joined by several women from the encampment who quickly went to the sides of the injured and helped Elly, thankful for her work. She stood and walked to Reuben's side, glancing to a small cluster of women who had recognized their family member from the clothing or other items nearby, and had already started their weeping.

"Let's leave them to their work," suggested Reuben, his hand on Elly's arm to encourage her to return with him to their horses. "We've got to tend to some of our kills."

As they rode up to the four downed buffalo, several women were already at work dressing out the animals. One woman saw them come near and stood, smiling and came before Elly and Reuben, "I am White Cloud. Kani-ache said we were to do this," motioning back to the animals, "that these were for our people."

Reuben and Elly smiled, and nodded, as Elly answered, "That's right. We just want a bit for ourselves, maybe a backstrap or two, but the rest is for you."

White Cloud smiled, looking from Reuben to Elly, "We are grateful." She looked directly at Reuben, "I remember when you came for us after the Comanche took us. If it were not for you, I would be a slave of the Comanche," she angrily spat the word 'Comanche' and paused, gaining her composure and smiled, "I am grateful." She had spoken of the time the summer before when Elly and others had been taken in a raid by the Comanche and Reuben had pursued and rescued the women.

Reuben just nodded, looked up to see Kaniache approach. He crossed his forearms on the pommel and looked at the war chief, "Well, your people have a lot of meat."

"Yes, but it was a costly hunt." He turned toward the site of the carnage caused by the stampede, "My people said you," looking at both Reuben and Elly, "helped them with those that were injured." He looked at the carcasses of the four buffalo, "And you took these for our people. You are a friend of the Mouache!"

"We *are* a friend of the Mouache, and we are proud to count the great Kaniache as our friend," replied Reuben. The chief nudged his mount closer, stretched out his arm toward Reuben and the men clasped forearms in the sign of friendship and nodded to one another.

Kaniache looked to the women busy at the carcasses, "Give our friends all that he asks for, the rest is his gift to you." The women all looked at their leader, nodding and smiling, and White Cloud began stripping the back straps of the young bull, preparing them for Reuben and Elly.

———

THE SUN WAS AT ITS ZENITH WHEN THEY RODE AWAY FROM the scene of the buffalo hunt. Atop the panniers were the two backstraps, bundled in a patch of hide, and secured to the packs. They rode in silence, thinking of the high cost of the hunt for the Mouache, three of their men had given their lives, two trampled in the trees, one overrun as he chased after the herd, his horse stumbling and throwing him under the feet of the stampeding herd. But such was the way of the native people. It was necessary for them to have the hunts, one in the early summer, one late fall, to provide for their people, and using every possible part of the taken animals, their tribe would be sustained for another year. It was a hard life, but a life of independence and freedom that followed in the way of their fathers and the custom of their people.

"It is sad for the families when they lose someone like that, but the tribe does so much to take care of their families. That is not often seen among the 'civilized' people," observed Elly, remembering the sadness in the eyes of the surviving family members.

"But you know, if people, the 'civilized' ones that is, would just follow the teachings of the Bible, they would take care of one another. But so many get caught up in taking care of themselves and seeking to make their fortune, they either trample over others, or pass them by, without even giving them a thought. And we don't even need to talk about those like the ones were chasing, that seem to think they can just take from others whenever they please," answered Reuben.

"Do you really think we'll find them at that ranch?" asked Elly, looking at her man.

"We'll know soon enough. We'll prob'ly get there

about dusk, maybe make camp up in the trees and watch the ranch from a distance 'fore we do anything." He glanced to the side to see Elly's expression. She rode quietly, thoughtful, turned to look at Reuben, nodded and smiled. "So, we can have some fresh back strap for supper?"

"Of course, I'm lookin' forward to that!" he declared, rubbing his belly like he was hungry and smiling mischievously at his wife.

"Sheriff! Sheriff! Sheriff!" shouted the lone rider that came into town at a full gallop, shouting and waving as he rode to the sheriff's office, skidded his horse to a stop as he swung down to the ground, shouting at the open door.

Sheriff Jack Sparks came to the door, frowning and taking a linen napkin from his collar with one hand as he held a chicken leg with the other, "What's all the shoutin' about!" he answered, taking another bite as he looked at the exasperated and excited man stumbling up onto the boardwalk.

"They got one! They got one!" he stammered, bending over with hands on his knees, fighting for a breath.

"Got one what?" asked Sparks, frowning at the man as he wrapped the partially eaten chicken leg in the napkin and wiping his mouth with the bundle.

"One o' them rebel rampagers! He's at the old Thirty-Nine-Mile station there by mountain, you know, the one that sits back off the road?" he breathed deep, stood erect and continued, "He came in last night, slept in the barn, and they found him there this mornin', but they didn't let on like they knew who he was. He had a horse, but it had gone lame and they're gonna try to keep him there till you get there!"

The sheriff motioned the man into his office, looked up and down the street and followed him inside. He motioned for the man to take a seat in the ladder back chair that sat near the pot-belly stove, and he stood before him, "Now, you're sure it's one o' them raiders?"

"Yeah! The station keeper, Burke, sent me an' said for you to hurry up with your posse!"

"An' there's just one of 'em?"

"Ummhmm, just the one. Think they said his name was Holl ... holli ... Holloman! That's it!"

The sheriff scowled at the man, nodded, "You go on over to the hotel, get John Murdock, tell him what's up, tell him to get some others, and we'll go after him!"

The messenger smiled, nodded, and took off up the street at a run. Within a short while, eight men rode up in front of the sheriff's office, led by Murdock, who hollered, "Hey sheriff! Get out here! We gotta get a move on if we're gonna make it back 'fore dark!"

The sheriff was buckling his belt around his expansive middle as he stepped out of the office. He grabbed his new Spencer rifle that stood beside the door and jammed it into the scabbard and swung aboard his waiting mount. He turned to face the others, "Raise your right hand!" as he lifted his beside his shoulder. Within moments he had sworn the posse in with the oath of a deputy and waved for the men to follow as he left the office on Front Street in a grand display of leadership, galloping from the office, bound for the stage station.

———

THE LOWERING SUN HAD JUST TUCKED ITSELF AWAY
bringing on the dim light of dusk when the posse
returned, jubilant at their success in 'capturing' the
outlaw who rode astraddle of a borrowed mule led by
the man Murdock. He rode beside the sheriff and
suggested, "Let's take him o'er to the livery. We can make
him talk there!"

"What's so important about makin' him talk?" asked
the uncertain sheriff.

"Don'tcha wanna find out where the others are?"

"Well, yeah, I s'pose. But I reckon they're done outta
the territory!"

"But, what about all that money? Ever'body said they
didn't take nuthin' with 'em when they lit out after the
posse hit their camp, an' they prob'ly hid it somewhere!
That's a lotta money they got! Some folks think they got
more'n a hunnert thousand dollars in gold!"

The sheriff frowned at the man. Murdock had a bit of
a shady reputation in town, although he ran the hotel, he
was known to do anything and everything to get his
hands on money, especially when it belonged to some
else and he did not have to work for it! The sheriff shook
his head, turned to look at the others and recognized
most of them were cohorts of Murdock, and reluctantly
agreed to the trip to the livery.

———

NINETEEN MILE RANCH LAY ASTRADDLE OF CURRANT
Creek where Smith Gulch came from the
mountains to the west. With fertile lands in the creek
bottom, the ranch house and barn sat near the trees in
the middle of the basin. Reuben recognized the terrain
and the dog-leg bend in the creek that was upstream

from the ranch house. He motioned toward the timbered ridge that pushed into the valley, and nudged Blue into the scattered Juniper. They crossed over a saddle, dropped into Smith Gulch and crossed the sandy bottomed draw before taking to the hills that rose south of the gulch and stood well above the ranch, offering a sufficient overlook for their watching the ranch.

"Looks like they're stayin' in the barn. They came from the house, so I believe they're takin' their meals in the house, and I don't see anything that says they're leaving, but we can't take a chance on them getting away." He paused, looking around their cold camp, the horses were stripped of their gear and things were stacked in the nook beneath the rocks where they would probably roll out their blankets. He glanced to the sky and the fading light of dusk, "Let's have somethin' to eat and I'll keep watch below as long as there's light."

"Too bad we can't broil up some of that fresh buffalo steak!" replied Elly, turning to go to the packs and fetch some of the smoked meat and left-over biscuits. She glanced over her shoulder at Reuben who stood peering through the branches of the juniper.

From their camp they could see the road leading into the ranch house and the lower pastures, but not the buildings. But his expression said he was thinking out their plan, what would be the safest and surest way of taking the Confederates. He shook his head as he thought about the men, men who probably entered the fight of the war and ended up being led astray into the possibility of self-enrichment. As he considered the men, picturing what might have been their life before the conflict, perhaps much like his with his family on the farm in Michigan. A family living in peace, building a future, making a life, to have it all destroyed by the evils of the war. Yet each man makes his own choices, his was to live a life as he had been raised, doing right by others and taking care of your own. It was never the way of his family to take from others or to intentionally do harm to others. His mother had been the guiding light with her unfailing faith in the Lord and persistence at instilling those values into her children.

He shook his head at the thought and the remembrance, glanced at Elly as she gathered the few items that would make their meal, and smiled at his good fortune in having such a good woman to stay by his side always, even when things were far from easy. There had been little sitting by the fire, or rocking on the porch for them, but they had always been together, and the good Lord willing, they would be together for many years to come. That was what was troubling him, that she might be put in danger, and he could not abide that, but what else could be done?

They sat side by side under the overhang of the rocks, watching the horses and mule snatching mouthfuls of grass and chewing in their own jaw swiveling way. Bear sat at their feet, waiting for a scrap to be tossed his way as he cocked his head to the side to give his usual mournful beggarly look. Elly grinned, tossed him a tidbit which he gratefully caught and quickly swallowed, only to look for another. "You ever notice how animals are just like people, you know, they get a little and want more!" she chuckled. "Or maybe its people being more like animals, never satisfied, always wanting more."

"Yeah, maybe, but right now I'm gonna take another look, see what I can figure out about what's next." He rose, watched as she stood beside him, and they embraced.

She pulled away, leaning back to look at her man, saw his contemplative expression and knew he was concerned about the coming confrontation. But she was committed and would stand beside him, no matter the cost. "Whatever it takes, that's what we'll do!"

Reuben nodded, dropped his eyes and turned away to return to the promontory that overlooked the ranch. Stepping through the juniper and oak brush, he bellied down beside a scraggly piñon and lifted the binoculars for one last look before the light faded. Three of the men were sitting outside the big front door of the barn, talking and fidgeting with something they passed back and forth. But when a lucifer flamed, Reuben realized they were sharing the new Durham loose tobacco to roll their own cigarettes. He chuckled at how people are so easily convinced of new practices but continued to watch the men until the others joined them, coming from within the barn. There was nothing about their behavior that suggested they were readying to leave, but when one of the men, his arm in a sling, brought out a pocket watch, flipped it open and spoke to the men, they all rose and went into the barn. Reuben immediately suspicioned the display of the watch told the men it was late, and they would rise early so they should turn in, because there is not much else to convince grown men to turn in for the night except to know they would be rising early. It was time for the two of them to lay out their plan.

The rising sun was just beginning to paint the clouds and mountain tops with color when Elly dropped off the hillside to take Smith Gulch into the bottom of Currant Creek valley. Aboard her appaloosa and leading the pack mule, she pointed her mount toward the ranch house that lay in the shadow of the foothills on the east. As she started down the road to the house, she spotted one man carrying a bucket on his way to the home. She guessed he was either the owner of the ranch or one of the ranch hands.

One man stepped from the small bunkhouse, stood on the stoop and stretched, arching his back and stretching his suspenders over his faded red union suit. He spotted the rider coming down the roadway, frowned and turned to holler into the bunkhouse. He stepped aside as another man came out, sat down on the stoop and worked at pulling his boots on, tugging at the straps and looking to the side at the approaching rider. "That's a woman!" he declared, jumping to his feet, and stomping his boots to finish getting them on his big feet.

The first man stepped off the little stoop, stood with

thumbs behind his suspenders, and greeted the rider, "Mornin'!"

Elly grinned, nodded, "Mornin'!" she looked at the men, glanced to the house and the barn and asked, "Think I might get some breakfast here'bouts?"

"Uh, prob'ly, ain't never seen Mrs. Byers turn anybody away, but ..." he answered, stubbing his toe in the ground and looking up at Elly, "What's a woman doin' out'chere all by your lonesome?" he bent to the side to look back up the road to see if there were any other riders and seeing none, he looked back to Elly for an answer.

"Oh, well, you know how it is, so many men off to war us women have to take care of things our ownselves." She smiled, nodding to the men, her elbow on the pommel as her free hand was tucked into her jacket, grasping her Colt.

"Uh, that's too bad." He grinned again, stepped forward to grab the rein of her horse to keep her from moving, the skittish animal had a way of dancing to the side every now and then. "I'm Burr an' that's Jerome," nodding to the man who stood agape on the stoop.

"Pleased to meet you men, I'm Elly. Are you men the owners?"

"Oh, no! We're just ranch hands, both of us been here with the Byers and Youngs, they're the owners, we been here goin' on six year. Step on down ma'am, Mrs. Byers is fixin' breakfast now and I'm sure she'd be mighty happy to have comp'ny!"

Elly looked around, "How 'bout you goin' in and tellin' her I'll be in shortly. I better put my horse and mule in the barn, maybe fork 'em some hay, if that's alright?"

"Sure, sure, but Jerome'll do that for ya!" He turned to look at his partner, "Won'tcha Jerome?"

"Sure, sure," he answered as he stepped away from the door.

"Oh, that's alright. Daisy here gets mighty skittish around men and likes to bite and kick." She wrinkled her nose as she leaned down to stroke the mare's neck. "I'll put her away and be right in," she stated, reining the appaloosa toward the barn.

"Suit'churself," mumbled Burr, glancing to his partner and shaking his head. "Women!"

"Ummhmm," replied Jerome, "Let's get us some breakfast!"

As Elly approached the barn which sat back to the north about fifty yards from the house, she heard men talking and readied herself. Keeping her hand on her pistol that was obscured by her buckskin jacket, she stopped before the door, slipped the Henry from the scabbard and stepped down, cradling her rifle in an unthreatening manner in the crook of her arm. With the reins trailing behind, loosely held by her right hand, she stepped through the door and spoke up, "Mornin' men!"

Her greeting startled the men who were saddling their horses, standing before the stalls. They turned, looking at the newcomer, most having to look over the saddles of the horse beside them. The man in front, who was struggling with his tack because of a sling on one arm, turned and glared at Elly, demanding, "Who're you?!"

Elly chuckled, smiled, and said, "I'm Elly. Who're you?"

The other men chuckled at the awkwardness of their leader, and laughed and one answered, "Why that's Jim, don'tcha know? Ain't that right, Jim?" prompting the others to laugh.

He growled back at Elly, "What're you doin' here?"

"I'm putting my horse up, gonna fork him some hay, then I'm goin' inside for breakfast. That alright with you, *Jim*?" she asked, smiling and cocking her head to the side.

"What's the matter boss, you feelin' threatened?" asked the man nearest to the leader.

"Shut-up! Get your gear on and get ready! We got breakfast to eat and places to go!" He growled and turned back to his gear.

Elly led the mare and mule to the opposite side of the barn, doing her best to look calm and disinterested, but occasionally glanced to the men and movement behind them. She slapped a rein over the top rail of the stall, turned slightly toward the men and waited, her rifle held across her chest at the ready.

The men were busy with their gear and had not paid much attention to Elly, although she heard a couple of them asking, "What's a woman doin' here?"

"Dunno, but I reckon we'll find out at breakfast!" snickered the answer.

"That's right boys, now stop what you're doing and face me, hands up!" demanded the familiar voice of Reuben. Bear stood beside him, jowls snarling as a low growl came from deep in his chest. He was standing with head lowered just below his shoulders, eyes watching the men, showing he was ready to attack if called upon. Reuben had come into the barn from the back, Bear at his side, for they knew if he had been with Elly, he would have been more protective and might give them away. Reuben had slipped in when their attention was focused on the woman. The men froze, looking around. Reynolds started to grab for his rifle that hung in the scabbard, but Reuben barked, "DON'T!" At the same time, Elly jacked a shell into the chamber of the Henry, a familiar sound that caught the attention of the men. They looked into the shadows as Elly stepped closer, the light from the big door showing her grin as she held the rifle at her hip, the muzzle pointed at the men.

"If you think you can take cover behind the horses, go ahead and try, but I've seen what spooked horses can do to a man crawling between his hooves and it ain't purty!" stated Reuben as he glanced from man to man and barked, "Hands up!"

"Now, walk out here in the open and belly down, be quick about it!" he growled. His was a voice that bespoke authority and demanded obedience. The men glanced from one to the other and slowly walked away from their horses. The one known as Harvey Briggs looked at the ground of the barn, saw some fresh cow pies from the milk cow, and tried to step aside, but Reuben ordered, "DOWN!" and the man went to his knees and whined, "I ain't layin' in that!" nodding toward the fresh manure.

"Then scoot to the side but get down 'fore I knock you down!" demanded Reuben.

With the attention focused on Briggs, Jim Reynolds glanced at Elly and back to Reuben. When Reuben looked toward Elly, Reynolds lunged for Reuben, but the distance was a few steps too far which allowed time for Reuben to drop the hammer on his Henry, the bullet grazing the side of Reynolds head and causing him to stumble to his knees and fall forward on his face. Bear had lunged at the man and at Reuben's call, had stood at Reynold's head, growling but not attacking. Reuben took a step back as he jacked another round into the Henry, and growled at the others, "Try it! Come on, try it!" he dared, snarling his lip and shaking his head.

The remaining men looked from Reuben to the dog and slowly complied, mumbling all the while and looking from Reuben to Elly and to their leader who was on the ground, one hand to his head and moaning. It was Jackson Robinson that said, "Hey! I remember you! You were the ones on a honeymoon, back in the canyon!"

Elly grinned, "We're still on our honeymoon," and glanced to Reuben, "ain't we honey?"

Reuben chuckled, "Yup, shore are!" He looked at the men, "Now stretch out your arms to your sides like you were an eagle that wanted to fly!" He watched each man do as he was told but Jim Reynolds, coming to his feet, complained, "I can't! I'm wounded!"

"Ummhumm, and I'm the one that wounded you! Now do as your told or I'll do it!"

With a nod to Elly that signaled her to watch the men, Reuben leaned his Henry on the stall siding and grabbed several pieces of rope and leather. He began with the man furthest from the door and twisted his hands behind his back and bound them tight. Elly kept her eyes on each of the others and when Reynolds tried to twist around to see what was happening, she ordered, "Keep your face flat or we'll move you closer to the cow patty and let you smell it up close!"

It was just enough of a distraction for Harvey Briggs as he thought, *She's a woman, she won't shoot!* And jumped to his feet, charging toward Elly, but Elly made a slight sidestep and brought the butt of the Henry flat against Brigg's face, having to tiptoe to reach him, but she put all her strength and weight behind the blow and stopped the man mid-stride. He grabbed at his smashed nose and split lip as he staggered back, growling, and grumbling something about a woman until Elly said, "Next time, I won't smack you, I'll just be done with you and put a bullet right between your eyes. But I expected one of you to try me, and now you know, so I'm guessin' we won't have any more trouble out of you, am I right?" she asked, looking from one to the other.

Reuben jerked up on Andrews' arm to crimp it behind him and growled, "She asked you a question. Are we gonna have any more trouble from you? Or do you want to have that cow pie for breakfast?"

Several of the men groaned at the thought of having their face next to a fresh cow pie, but none chose to move, all mumbling their agreement. Within moments, all were bound tight, and Reuben began lifting them to their knees and motioning for them to move to the side, "Sit right there!" pointing to the fence rail. While Elly continued to guard them, Reuben checked each mount, ensuring the saddles were on and secure, then led each one outside the barn and tethered them at a hitchrail. When all the horses were there, he brought each man out, helped him aboard his horse, then tied their feet together under the belly of the horse.

When all the men were mounted, he tied the reins of each horse to the tail of the next horse, until they were lined out, one after the other. As he was finishing, a voice hollered from the front of the house, "Hey! What's goin' on there!" and three men started toward the barn. Elly stepped from beside the lead horse, held her rifle toward the three and Reuben answered, "I'm Deputy Marshal Reuben Grundy, and I'm taking these men back to Fairplay for trial!"

"Why? What'd they do?" asked the one man who Elly recognized as the man who carried the bucket into the house and assumed he was the owner, Byers.

"They killed several men, robbed several stages and stations, and more. But that's for a trial to determine," answered Reuben. He turned to face the main road and split the air with a piercing whistle that sounded like the scream of an eagle. He turned back to the three men who stood staring, and explained, "I'm just calling for my other deputies."

Within moments the big blue roan came trotting down the road with a big black dog at his side. The three men looked from the horse and dog to the man standing with his Henry held loosely at his side, and Byers asked, "Deputies?"

"The best kind!" he answered, smiling. When Blue trotted to his side, Reuben grabbed the reins, swung aboard and with the Henry on the rebels, he nodded to Elly. She smiled, went into the barn for her appy and the mule, returned and mounted up, holstering her Henry. Reuben looked at her and asked, "You wanna lead or follow?"

She smiled, nudged the appy toward the road and snatched up the lead of the first horse and started up the road. The three men stood staring at the single file of riders leaving the ranch, Byers shaking his head when the screen door slammed and a woman with a wide apron stepped out, wiping her hands on her apron, and asked, "What's goin' on?

"You ain't gonna believe it Ma, you ain't," answered the older man as he turned to the house. He asked, "Got'ny more coffee?"

31 / JOURNEY

They had traveled only about two miles before the men started complaining. They were passing the mouth of Horsethief Gulch when Reynolds complained, "We can't keep ridin' like this! This is all-fired painful! My legs are hurtin', he tied my wrists too tight, can't hardly keep my balance ..." he shook his head as Elly totally ignored his pleas. She was leading the bunch, Bear out in front on scout, and the long lead line from the halter of the first horse was dallied around her saddle horn. She glanced back at the string of horses and riders, shook her head and turned back to the trail.

"Hey! I'm talkin' to you! Ain't you got no compassion?" whined Reynolds.

Elly glanced over her shoulder, shook her head, "Crybaby! Why didn't you have compassion on all those men you killed?"

"That's different! This is torture!" sniveled Reynolds, and two or three of the men behind him muttered their agreement but their words were unintelligible.

"When'r we gonna get sumpin' to eat?" cried Harvey

Briggs, prompting the three behind him, Jackson Robinson, John Andrews, and Thomas Knight, to echo his plea.

"If you don't shut up, we'll ride all the way to Fairplay without stopping, much less give you anything to eat!" hollered Reuben from the end of the line.

The men grumbled, squirming in their saddles trying to get more comfortable. Once chastised, the men settled into a quiet acceptance and the only sounds were the creak of saddle leather, the shuffling of horses' hooves and the occasional clatter of hooves on rocks. Elly watched a pair of ospreys circling what appeared to be a nest in the top of a scraggly cottonwood near the creek. She heard their high-pitched peeps as they circled and one spread their wings and with a few flaps, landed atop the brush pile of a nest. Something caught Elly's eye just beyond the treetop and she shaded her eyes for a better look. High up on the shoulder of a timber covered hill, three natives sat their horses watching the string of horses and riders in the valley below. Elly turned to look back down the line, and while Reuben watched, she nodded, pointing with her chin toward the natives. He nodded and grinned, indicating he had spotted them.

A few miles further and the road bent away from Currant Creek to take to a higher basin that was open and lay below the crest of the higher foothills. The steady gait of the horses, the easy rocking in the saddle, and the bobbing head of the horses was a little mesmerizing and caused Elly to relax. Her chin hitting her chest brought her full awake just as Jim Reynolds had kicked his horse, causing him to lunge ahead and bring him beside Elly. Reynolds guided his mount with his knees, trying to get the big black to drive against the smaller appaloosa mare of Elly, but the appy was a sure-footed mountain bred horse that came from the natives and had been used to hunt buffalo. When the bigger mount tried to shoulder the appy from the trail, Elly grabbed the reins, jabbed her heels to the ribs of the appy, and they jumped away from the black. The move caught the black off balance causing him to stumble and Elly drove the appy against the shoulder to the black, causing him to trip and fall to his shoulder, eliciting a scream from the terrified Reynolds.

Both horses fought for footing, the black coming to his feet and stumbling to the side, Jim Reynolds dangling to the side and slipping lower, startling the horse who started crow-hopping until Elly pulled the lead line tight, dallied it around the saddle horn and gave the black something to stabilize himself and he struggled to find sure footing and began to settle down. Reuben had quickly come to the side of the ruckus and reached down to grab Reynolds by the binding on his wrists and pulled him back into his saddle.

While Reuben tended to Reynolds, Elly had slipped her Henry from the scabbard and barked, "Don't try it!" gaining the others attention and keeping them from trying anything. When Reynolds horse had broken away, the lead from the second horse had pulled free from its tail and now stood, shaking his head at the sharp jerk suffered from the breakaway. Elly kept her rifle on the others in line, preventing any further attempts to escape. Reuben stepped down, and retied the leads to tails, checked each one and stroked the horses' necks, talking to them and settling them down.

Reuben walked back to the side of Reynold's horse, put his hand on animal's neck and looked up at Reynolds. In a low and steady voice, he explained, "You try that again, and we won't even try to stop your horse from taking off at a run. We might even shoot a little to scare it more, and then watch as he drags you along this road, bouncing your hard head off the rocks and leaving a trail of blood and brains. How's that sound? Wanna try it? I'll slap him now if you want!"

"No, no, no. I'll stay in line, no, I will, really!" he pleaded, prompting a grin from Reuben as he nodded to Elly and walked back to climb aboard Blue.

It was approaching mid-day when they broke into the open and the road showed the rolling hills of the flats and the long high timber covered ridge of Thirty-Nine Mile Mountain. This was the scene of the buffalo hunt but the only thing remaining were a few carrion eaters picking at the left-over gut piles. There was no obvious sign of the Mouache and when the road hung on the downslope of the big mountain, they could see the distant Three-Mile Mountain that sat just beyond their previous campsite. Reuben and Elly had talked earlier about where they would stop for nooning and had agreed on a spot next to the headwaters of Currant Creek where the horses would have ample water and graze, and there would be shade for a brief camp, maybe a fire for some coffee.

To their right, the long slope that rose to the timbered crest of the ridge showed sign of the buffalo passing, but in the low swale of the creek bottom, the grass and water beckoned. But Elly lifted her hand to her brow and stood in the stirrups to look up the road where a bit of a dust cloud was rising. She turned to look back to Reuben, motioning him forward and he trotted Blue to her side, "What'chu see?" he asked.

"Not sure, but it's raisin' a dust cloud," she nodded to the north end of the valley toward the crest of Currant Creek Pass. He shaded his eyes, looking as did Elly, and turned to retrieve his binoculars from the saddle bags.

With the field glasses shaded by his hat because of the bright midday sun, he began to grin and dropped the binoculars to turn to Elly. "It's the cavalry!"

"The cavalry?" she asked, frowning. "What are they doin' here?"

"I'm thinkin' they're lookin' for these fellas," nodding to the men sitting uncomfortably aboard restless horses.

"Well as far as I'm concerned, if they want 'em, they are welcome to 'em!" Elly glanced to the creek bed, and motioned, "How 'bout we go down there and wait for 'em?"

Reuben nodded, looked back at the men and let Elly lead the string off the road and into the grass. Reynolds looked at Reuben and asked, "What's goin' on? Who's that comin'?"

"Looks like the cavalry. I'm guessin' it's Lieutenant Shoop of Company A, 3rd Colorado Cavalry, made up of mostly volunteers that hang out around Fairplay and Buckskin. But I do believe the Colonel out of Golden City and the Governor's office, I think his name is Chivington, has been wantin' the captain to get involved in the hunt for Confederate sympathizers and such."

"Sympathizers!? We're not sympathizers, we're regular troops of Company A, Wells Battalion, Third Texas Regiment under General Douglas Hancock Cooper!" spouted Reynolds, prompting nods and agreement from the other men.

"Yeah, and I'm General Ulysses S. Grant!" sputtered Reuben, stepping down and taking Blue and Daisy to water while Elly watched the prisoners. Once their horses had their fill, he led them upstream and picketed them on the grass. Walking back to the prisoners, he explained, "I'm gonna get you down, one at a time and sit you well apart from one another. Then I'll water the horses, and let each of you go to the bushes, one at a time."

"'Bout time!" muttered Harvey Briggs, watching Reuben untie Reynold's feet and slide him off his saddle. He sat Reynolds down in the grass, then proceeded to unhorse the others, sitting them apart from one another. With Elly still watching them with her Henry at the ready, he took the horses to water, picketed the animals and returned for the men. He lifted Reynolds to his feet, but the man stumbled around, falling into Reuben and hollered to the others, "Now!"

The four other men rolled to their knees and fought to get up, but Elly fired a round at their feet, jacked another round into the chamber as she hollered, "On your bellies, NOW!"

Reynolds had tried to push Reuben into the brush, but Reuben stepped to the side, hooked his boot at Reynolds ankle and with one hand at the back of his neck, drove him to the ground. He tried to roll away, but Reuben dropped, driving his knee into Reynolds back and drew his Remington pistol, cocking it and sticking the muzzle into Reynold's ear, "Go ahead, try to outrun this bullet!" he snarled.

Reynolds lay completely still and muttered, "I still need to go to the bushes!"

"You're not going anywhere!" answered Reuben. He stood, stepping back from the leader of the group, keeping his pistol trained on him as he looked to Elly and glanced to the other men. "Reckon we'll just wait for the Cavalry!"

"Suits me!" answered Elly, moving to a big flat-top rock to take a seat, keeping her rifle on the outlaws. Bear came to her side and bellied down beside her, watching the men and with his tongue lolling and drool dripping, he looked like he wanted one of the men to try to get away just so he could have a bite of fresh meat.

As Reuben suspected, it was Lieutenant Shoop and the Third Colorado that stopped on the road and with a raised hand, the captain and one other officer, a Lieutenant, rode their horses down into the grass where the small group waited, and stepped down. He looked at Reuben and Elly, tipped his hat to the lady, then looked at the men and back to Reuben, "Are these the men you were looking for?" he asked.

"That's right. That one," pointing to the man still lying face down in the grass, "is Jim Reynolds, the leader, and that one," pointing to Harvey Briggs, "is Harvey Briggs, and the way I understand it, those two are related somehow. These others are Jackson Robinson, John Andrews, and Thomas Knight."

"I thought there were more of them?" asked the captain.

"We cut the trail of three others, but they went on the other side of that mountain, the road leads to Colorado City and beyond, but I think they're pretty well gone."

"Not necessarily. There was one, a Thomas Hollo-man, that was captured by the posse out of Fairplay, seems he was sleeping in the barn at a stage station, and they caught him and held him for the posse. They took him back to Fairplay, questioned him, hung him three times before he talked, then he told everything he knew. When the sheriff told me about this bunch that had come this way, and that he thought you were on their trail, well, Colonel Chivington replied by telegram and said I was to come after them."

Reuben grinned, glanced to Elly, and replied to the captain, "You are welcome to them, captain."

The captain began barking orders to his men and

they quickly had the outlaws back aboard their horses but retied their hands in front so they could hold onto the saddle horns. They did not tie their feet but put a length of rope around one man's neck, stretched it to the next and soon had the five men joined by a long dangling rope, a loop around each neck so that if one tried to flee, it would choke the others to death. Reuben chuckled as he watched the expression on each of the rebels faces, and as they started back to Fairplay, both Reuben and Elly waved at the men, smiling and chuckling as they rode out of sight.

Elly looked at Reuben, "So, you 'bout ready to have some fresh buffalo steak?"

"Am I!? You bet!" he replied, starting to the pack on the mule.

32 / FAIRPLAY

Reuben stripped the gear from each of the horses and the mule, stacking things under the overhang of the big willows. There was one big cottonwood and several saplings where he stretched out the blankets and prepared their beds. Elly was already busy with the steaks, hanging them over the flames on the green willow withes, while the pot bubbled with chunks of meat, timpsila, cattail shoots, and green onions, all freshly gathered from near the streambed. The stream was no more than a couple feet wide at it widest, and only about eight or ten inches deep, but it ran clear and cold. It was not their usual camp, except for the cover of willows, alders and the few cottonwoods, they were in the bottom of the swale and had little view of the surrounding area. Reuben stood looking and walked to the side of Elly. "If that's gonna be a while, I think I'll walk up on that little knob and have a look around." He nodded toward the bald rise about five hundred yards toward the big ridge.

Elly chuckled, knowing his penchant for wanting to know what was around, whether it be game, outlaws, or natives. She nodded, smiling, "Go ahead, but don't be too long. This won't take long," she declared touching his arm and looking up at him. He grinned, turned on his heel and started up the little slope to cross the roadway and make his way to the knob. He already had his Sharps and binoculars in hand, and he trotted the short distance, slowing only with the climb up the rise.

As he crested the little knob, he spotted a shady spot on the lee side of a scraggly cedar and seated himself, extracted the binoculars, and began his survey. Three big wolves, one black and two grey, had commandeered a big gut pile and were making a feast of the leftovers. Most of the other piles had been consumed, but several coyotes, ravens, one badger, and a golden eagle were making short work of the few remaining scraps. Away from the refuse and near the tree line higher up, Reuben saw something he could not make out. His first thought was that it was a lone buffalo that had been wounded and took off by himself to die alone. But when it moved, he watched closer, and it soon revealed itself to be a grizzly.

The hump at his shoulders, big head, and general size told Reuben it was a boar, and a big one. The big beast ambled along the tree line, moving to the south, and with a glance over his shoulder showed little interest in the offal of the buffalo kill. He had probably already eaten his fill and was bound for higher country. Reuben kept watching until he disappeared into the trees and as he lost sight of the bruin, Reuben let out a deep breath, his relief evident.

He scanned the crest of the ridge, knowing the camp of the Mouache Ute was just over the rise, but he saw no smoke or other sign. He thought they had already taken their leave, with travois laden with fresh meat, they would probably return to their summer encampment in the Wet Mountain Valley, near the cabin built by Reuben and Elly. He searched the valley in all directions, saw a couple mule deer, two cow elk with calves, a few more raggedy coyotes, but nothing else. Satisfied, he tucked away the binoculars and rose to return to the camp and the big meal Elly was fixing, his mouth watering at the thought.

"So, how long you fixin' to stay here?" asked Elly, dishing up some of the vegetable stew on Reuben's plate.

"Oh, maybe a week or two," answered Reuben, doing his best to keep a somber expression. "Nice place, don'tcha think?" he added, looking around the valley, keeping his eyes from Elly.

"Do you want me to hit you with the cast iron lid from the Dutch oven?" she asked, maintaining her composure, much like Reuben tried.

"Now, why'd you wanna do a thing like that?" he asked, accepting the plate from a smiling Elly.

"If you don't know, maybe I should hit you and knock some sense into that thick head!"

"Now woman! You want me to bend you over my knee and teach you some manners?"

"First off, you're too slow to catch me, and you're not big enough to spank me!" sticking out her tongue at him.

He chuckled, "I take it you're kinda anxious to see Estrella?"

"Ummhmm, and I'd also like to see how Levi and Precious are doing, and if possible, check on Maude."

"Think you could get all that done in time for us to make it back to our cabin 'fore snow falls?" chuckled Reuben, grabbing one of the steaks that simmered over the flames.

She lifted the cast iron lid as if she would throw it

and Reuben ducked, slipped off the rock, spilling his plate and his coffee, prompting both of them to break out in laughter. As they settled down, Elly picked up Reuben's plate and filled it up again, handing it to him as he found his seat and made himself comfortable, watching Bear make short work of the spilled stew. She giggled some more, started to pour his coffee but the giggling made the pot jiggle and she splashed some of the hot coffee on his leg, making him start to jump again, but instead just groaned and held his plate still. He looked at Elly and said, "Since it's not safe to stay here, maybe we better head out in the morning?" he asked.

"Just what I was thinking," she agreed, smiling and pouring her own cup of coffee.

———

MID-MORNING SAW THEM RIDING INTO FAIRPLAY, HEADED for the telegram office which sat next to the Platte Valley Mercantile. As they tied off the animals at the hitchrail, Reuben said, "Let's get the telegram off to the governor then we'll get us a room at the hotel and maybe have lunch with Estrella."

Elly smiled, nodding, "I'm anxious to see the girl. It seems a lot longer than it really was, but now that it's over, I'm ready to relax a mite." She paused, frowning, looked at Reuben, "What day is it?"

"Whaddya mean?"

"What day is it, you know, Monday, Tuesday, Wednesday?"

Reuben frowned, "Uh, I dunno. Let's see, it was a Saturday when we left here the first time, or was it Monday?" He shook his head, grinning, "Oh well, I'm sure the telegrapher will know."

They stepped inside, went to the counter as a man who was seated at a desk with the key was busy with a message. The shelf above the desk was full of the many batteries and wires necessary for the wire service. Reuben glanced around, saw a pad on the counter and picked up a pencil and began writing out the message. The telegrapher finished before Reuben and looked up at the couple at the counter, "Howdy folks! Be right wit'cha!"

Reuben was focused on his writing of the message, prompting Elly to answer, "That's alright." Nodded to Reuben and added, "He's still writing anyway!" and chuckled as she put her hand on his shoulder and stepped closer to his side.

Reuben pushed the paper across the counter and the telegrapher picked it up and began to read –

John Evans, Governor Colorado Territory
    Golden City, Co

Governor,
    Have captured five of Reynolds gang, including Jim Reynolds. Turned over to Lieutenant Shoop, 3rd Colorado. Two others dead, one released by Fairplay posse, two escaped to south, possibly Texas. Await your orders.
    Marshals Grundy, Fairplay

The telegrapher frowned, looked at Reuben, shook his head, "I ain't never had to send a telegram to the governor 'fore. An' you signed it Marshals, don'tchu mean Marshal?"

"Nope, send it as it is," he chuckled, "we're both marshals," nodding to Elly and looking back at the telegrapher.

"Alright, that'll be, uh," as he started counting the words.

"That'll be nothing – send it collect. The governor has more money than we do!"

The telegrapher chuckled, "Ya got that right!" and turned to his desk to begin sending. He looked up at Reuben and asked, "You wanna wait for a reply?"

"No, if one comes, we'll be at the hotel."

The telegrapher nodded, turned back to his key as Reuben and Elly left the office. Once outside, they stopped, looking around the town and Reuben said, "I think I'll stop by the sheriff's office, so if you want to go to the hotel and get us a room, I'll bring our gear and take the animals to the livery."

She smiled up at her man, "We still don't know what day it is!"

Reuben chuckled, "Ask 'em at the hotel, they should know. But, I think it's Saturday, maybe."

Elly grinned back and said, "Don't wait another week to come to the hotel!"

"And you said his name was Holloman?" asked Reuben, looking across the desk at sheriff Jack Sparks.

"That's right. After Murdock got his men together and made up the posse, we made a quick trip to Thirty-Nine Mile Station and picked him up. When we got back, Murdock and his men were determined to get the man to talk an' tell where the others were, at least that's what they said, but what they really wanted to know was where they stashed the gold dust and money they stole."

"And did they?"

The sheriff harrumphed, "After what they done to that fella, I don't think you could believe a word he said! Why, if'n I'da been him I'da tol' 'em the moon was made o' cheese if'n that's what they wanted to know!"

"What'd they do?"

"They thunked on him a mite, then they put a rope on his neck, hauled him up to the rafters, most choked him to death, then dropped him on the ground. He coughed and choked some, wouldn't answer 'em and they done it again! Three times they done it!"!

"Why didn't you stop 'em? You're the sheriff!"

"Hah! Ever' man on that posse was one o' Murdock's men and they done what he wanted. Wouldn't one of 'em pay any attention to me!"

"Then what'd they do?"

"Wal, they let him talk a mite, tol' 'em what they wanted to hear. They had a man writin' it all down and when he was done, they let him go!"

"Just let him go? If you were sure he was one of the Reynolds gang, why didn't you put him in jail?"

The sheriff just shook his head, dropped his eyes to his desk and looked back up at Reuben with a mournful expression and breathed deep, lifting his shoulders in a shrug and looked back down at his folded hands. Reuben stared at the man for a moment, rose from his chair and with nothing more than a glance over his shoulder, left the Sheriff's office.

Elly was standing outside the hotel when Reuben came from the sheriff's office. She smiled at the sight of him and waited for him to draw near. "What for you waitin' outside? I thought you'd get us a room, find Estrella and ..." started Reuben, frowning. But the upheld hand of his woman stopped him.

"Estrella is not here, but before you get all upset, she left a message for us to join her in Buckskin!" explained Elly.

"Buckskin!? What's she doin' in Buckskin?"

"She didn't say, but I think we should do as she requested, and join her. Don't you?"

"Uh, yeah, I s'pose," he replied, looking longingly at the hotel as his thoughts of a warm bath and fresh clothes were rapidly disappearing. "I'll go get the horses," he mumbled as he turned away.

"I'll come with you, and we'll leave from there,"

replied Elly, tucking her hand through the crook of Reuben's arm to walk beside him. Fortunately, he had yet to bring the gear and packs from the livery to the hotel and all were waiting in a pile beside the stalls near the horses. The smithy was busy at his forge as they walked in, but he nodded as they passed. In a short while, the horses were saddled, the mule loaded, and they started from the livery, stopping to talk to the smithy before leaving.

"Say, smithy, there was a friend of ours that was here about a week or so ago, said he was gonna go to work for you, name of Levi. He still around?" asked Reuben.

The smithy smiled, shook his head, "No, reckon not. He was only here a couple days when the livery man from Buckskin came in, wantin' to sell his livery. We struck a deal, included Levi in the bargainin' and he took over the shop in Buckskin. He's workin' on shares, and if things go well, he'll own the place in a couple years or so. Good man, that," explained the smithy, smiling at the thought of his new friend and partner.

Reuben grinned, glanced to a smiling Elly, and agreed with the smithy. "How much do we owe you?"

"You weren't here long enough to charge for anything but the hay and grain, so four bits oughta cover it," offered the smithy. Reuben dug some coin from his pocket, sorted it out and gave the man a half-dollar coin, prompting a smile from the smithy who jammed it into his pocket and with a nod to Reuben, turned back to his work.

Buckskin was only about ten miles from Fairplay. With a trail that sided the Middle Fork of the South Platte River, they passed London Junction and as they came to Alma, they took a well-traveled road that bent to the west into the valley of Buckskin Creek that lay between two snow-capped peaks of what some were calling the Mosquito Range. Buckskin was more of a bustling town than Fairplay with four hotels, several stores, and saloons and taverns too numerous to mention. The mines throughout the Buckskin valley had proven prosperous with the Phillips mine alone producing over a half-million dollars of gold in 1861 and 1862. But there was some confusion within the town that had its name changed from Buckskin to Laurette, but most still called it Buckskin.

"It was just last year that we were here and look at all the new buildings!" declared an amazed Elly, giving a sweeping motion with her arm to indicate the busy town. "There's the Pacific Hotel, are we staying there again?"

"Might as well, at least we know the place. Did Estrella say where to meet her?" asked Reuben, giving a tug on the lead rope of the mule who had become a little skittish with all the activity.

"The hotel clerk said he heard her talking with young Sharman, that boy who was flirting with her, and they said somethin' about the Tabor store. You remember, Horace and Augusta Tabor, Reverend Dyer introduced us, and I stayed with her while you were off chasing those Espinosas."

"Well, even though it's a bustlin' town, it's a lot like any other small town and I'm bettin' its one of those everybody knows everybody kinda towns. So, I reckon the Tabors would know where she is if anybody knows." He looked about, up and down the street, and nodded, "There's their store yonder," pointing with his chin, "the one with the flag and sign that says *Post Office.*"

Reining up in front of the store, they both stepped down and Reuben wrapped the reins of both horses and the mule around the hitchrail while Elly, anxious to see Estrella, wasted no time in going inside to ask about the girl. After telling Bear to wait with the horses, Reuben followed Elly into the store, paused for his eyes to become accustomed to the dim interior, and saw Elly hugging Estrella beside the counter. Estrella turned and held out her arms for Reuben to give her a hug and he obliged. When they stepped away from the counter, Estrella began chattering like a nest full of hungry baby birds and Elly said, "Whoa, whoa. Slow down, there's plenty of time for us to catch up, so, how 'bout coming with us while we get us a room and then we'll plan for lunch or something?"

Estrella smiled, looked back to Augusta Tabor, and looked again at Elly, "I need to help Mrs. Tabor here for a bit, then I can come have lunch with you."

"Fine, we'll be at the Pacific, and we can eat at the dining room there. Give us enough time to get cleaned up, then meet us there," the two women were standing facing one another, clutching each other's hands.

"I will," answered Estrella, squeezing Elly's hands and turning back to the counter.

———

THE BUCKSKIN LIVERY AND BLACKSMITH WAS NEAR THE end of the main street on the upper end of the town, but only a couple blocks from the hotel. Reuben had carried their haversack, bedrolls, rifles and scabbards, and saddle bags into the hotel where Elly secured them a room and made arrangements for hot baths. While Reuben took the animals to the livery, she had the manager carry the gear to their room and began to prepare for her bath.

The livery was a large barn with attached corrals and

the blacksmith forge, anvil and other accouterments were just inside the main door. The ring of hammer on steel sounded like a clarion as it echoed down the street, the broad shoulders shone with perspiration, while the big hammer lifted and dropped on a molten piece of metal. Between strikes, Reuben said, "Hello Levi!"

The brawny man stopped in mid swing, looked at the man with the sun at his back and frowned, turned to the side to see his image better, and once recognized, a broad grin began to split his face. He thrust the hot metal in the tub, lay the hammer down and spread his arms wide to give Reuben a bear hug. There was no hesitation on the part of either man, for good friends do not concern themselves with trivialities but appreciate the presence of their friend. When the two men stepped back from one another, Reuben said, "You are lookin' mighty prosperous!" grinning.

Levi smiled, nodding, and said, "It's just like you said, the good Lord has blessed me more'n I ever imagined! The smithy, Ezra, in Fairplay he'ped set this up and it's, it's, well, more'n I ever thought possible! And I have you to thank for it!"

"I'm happy for you Levi. And how's your missus?"

"Precious is as precious as ever, and she's so happy she's singin' all the day long!" he chuckled, picturing his little woman in his mind's eye.

"We hope to see her before we go," stated Reuben, lifting his eyebrows in a question.

"You goin' to Rev'n Dyer's service t'morro? We be there!"

Reuben smiled, nodding, "If you tell me where it's goin' to be, we'll be there!"

"He hol's meetin's in the dance hall, next to the Laurette House."

"We'll be there!" answered Reuben. "Now, how 'bout a place for my animals?"

————

IT WAS OBVIOUS THAT ESTRELLA'S EXCITEMENT WAS boiling over as she could not sit still and fussed with napkins, place ware, everything in front of her, until the waitress had taken their order and left the table. She smiled at Reuben and Elly and began, "It's so exciting, I don't know where to start, but Johnathan, you remember him, his father Mr. Sharman, had the Platte Valley Mercantile in Fairplay," as she spoke, she nodded her head and looked from Reuben to Elly and continued, almost without a breath. "Johnathan and his father have invested in a new store here in Buckskin. Mr. C.W. Kitchen came from Cañon City and will put in this store, another in California Gulch, and others. But he wants Johnathan to run this one, and Johnathan wants me to help him! Isn't that exciting? I've been helping Mrs. Tabor in their store, and I also helped in the store in Fairplay, but I'm excited about helping with a new store! And Johnathan," she sighed as she mentioned his name but continued, "he's so wonderful. We've spent so much time together and, well, we just want to be together. And I can board with Mrs. Tabor and help her as I'm needed, too!" She leaned back and caught her breath, looking from Reuben to Elly and back, then asked, "Well?"

Reuben frowned, looked from Estrella to Elly and back, "Well, what?"

"What do you think about my staying here and helping in the store?"

Elly frowned, "But Estrella, you hardly know the

boy!?" speaking the words in a statement but yet asking the question.

"But how long did you know Reuben before you got married?" she asked, having heard the story of the wagon train and escape from the natives, before.

"That's different," pleaded Elly, glancing to Reuben with an expression that looked as if she was floundering and needed a lifeline.

Reuben grinned, looked around and seeing the waitress, lifted his cup to ask for more coffee, then looked back at Elly and Estrella, smiling, but saying nothing.

Elly added, "And I was older than you are!" she declared, frowning.

"We're not getting married ... yet," answered Estrella, smiling coyly.

"What would your father say?" asked Reuben.

"That's easy, he would say what he has said before, 'Sigue a tu corazón', 'Follow your heart.'"

Reuben dropped his eyes, peeked up at Elly with a smile, then looked at Estrella, "So, I understand Preacher Dyer is having services in the morning, is that right?"

"Yes, yes he is!" she answered, excitedly. "John and I will help him set up later this afternoon."

"Good, good. Then how 'bout we finish this discussion tomorrow after we've had time to think and pray about it, would that be alright?"

Estrella smiled, appearing to be a little embarrassed, but nodded excitedly and looked up as the waitress brought their meals. It was a pleasant time of visiting, talking about what had happened in the last several days and what their plans might be in the days to come.

They were an impressive couple that caught every eye as they walked into the hall for the services of the Reverend John Dyer, also known as the Snowshoe Itinerant for his many travels among the gold camps delivering mail and packages in the middle of winter. Elly was in a long full skirt of black brocade that whirled about her feet as she moved, the lace ruffle at the hem accenting her movements. The wide cinched belt at her waist set off the lacy ruffled white cotton blouse that buttoned up to her neck where a lace collar stood with tiny bows all around. The waist length silk jacket added a distinguished air to the outfit and the matching thin brimmed hat sat atop her long blonde curls. Reuben's wool slacks hung beneath the crisp white cotton shirt that lay underneath his brocade waistcoat that matched Elly's dress. His long frock coat hung open and the length accented his tall lean frame. He had doffed his flat brimmed black hat when he entered the building and hung it on his boot toe when they were seated.

Estrella, Johnathan, and Johnathan's parents were seated beside one another taking up the remainder of seats in that row. As Reuben looked around, the crowd was quickly filling up the hall, the chairs in the rows left few seats open, the benches along the wall covered with prospectors and miners still in their usual work clothes.

Preacher Dyer had walked among the congregants, shaking hands and greeting everyone, asking about each one, getting acquainted with newcomers. When he spotted Reuben and Elly, he quickly made his way to their side, "Reuben, Elly! It's so good to see you! I was wondering when you might return." He smiled, glanced to Estrella and Johnathan, "I was beginning to think I would have to start brushing up on my wedding notes ..." and chuckled as Estrella blushed and looked away. "But she has, well, both of them have been a big help to me, setting up for the services and such. I appreciate the opportunity to get to know them both."

Reuben caught a bit of a look given by the preacher in the direction of Johnathan but knew this was not the time to discuss anything yet tucked it away in his mind to ask about at a later time. Preacher Dyer glanced to Reuben, gave a slight nod, and both men knew there was something to talk about. The preacher went on with his greeting, then mounted the platform and stood behind the pulpit, nodded to a woman at a portable organ, and said, "Let's all stand and sing *In the Sweet By-and-By.*" The woman began pumping with her feet and began playing. The preacher started singing, prompting the others to join in,

> There's a land that is fairer than day
> And by faith we can see it afar
> For the Father waits over the way
> To prepare us a dwelling place there.

In the sweet by and by, we shall meet on that
beautiful shore.

After singing two verses and the chorus three times, he motioned for everyone to be seated and stepped in front of the lectern and began, "Folks, I want to take my text from the book of Acts, chapter 16 and verse 30. The question is asked, 'Sirs, what must I do to be saved?' and I would like to ask you that same question this morning. This comes from the jailer in Philippi that tended the prison where Paul and Silas had been thrown, after ministering to the local workers. God chose to release them by bringing an earthquake that opened the prison and the jailor, thinking he would be killed for letting the prisoners escape, saw Paul and Silas had not escaped. He was so overcome, wanting to know the God that Paul served, and he asked this question, that I ask you today, *What must I do to be saved.*" He paused, looking around the crowd and continued, "Let me give you the same answer, *Believe in the Lord Jesus Christ, and thou shalt be saved, and thy house.*"

He stepped away from the lectern, leaned on it with his elbow and added, "That's not just believing in the existence of God and His son Jesus, it's believing *on.*" With another piercing look around the crowd, he continued, "Let's focus on that little word *on.*" He stepped closer to the crowd, pulled an unoccupied chair from the front row and set it beside the lectern. "You see that chair? How many of you believe that's a chair?" and looked around the crowd to see most hands raised. "Good, good. But do you believe that chair will hold you up?" again he looked for uplifted hands and most raised their hands.

He smiled, stepped close to the chair, "But, is that

chair holding you up right now?" he looked at many confused faces, and added, "And it's not holding me up either. But," and he stepped up on the chair to stand of the seat of the chair and looked out at the crowd, "Now it is holding me up. The difference? I am *on* the chair. You see the difference? Before I believed in the existence of the chair, and even believed it would hold me, but now I *trust* the chair and have put my entire weight on it by being *on* the chair. If it falls, I fall, if it stands, I stand. My complete trust is in the chair."

He stepped down, walked across the front of the crowd, looking directly into the faces of the nearest people, and then said, "Many people believe in God, in that He exists, but they have never *trusted* Him. That's what I'm asking you to do today, *Believe on the Lord Jesus Christ and thou shalt be saved, and thy house.*" He stepped back behind the lectern, "Now, all you need to do to trust Him or to believe *on* Him is to talk to Him. That's done by prayer, but it must be a prayer you believe with all your heart. Now, I'm going to pray a prayer, and if you want to trust Jesus, to believe *on* Him today, then say the prayer with me." He paused, bowed his head and began, "*Our precious Father, we come to you today to put our trust in you and you alone. Many here today want to believe on you and I will lead in prayer,*" he paused, and added, "Now if you want to do that today, then repeat this prayer after me, *Dear God, I want to trust you today to take me to Heaven when I die. Forgive me of my sins and come into my heart and save me. Thank you for saving me. In Jesus name, Amen.*" Throughout the crowd, many voices had joined in the prayer with the preacher, praying the prayer to put their trust in Jesus, and those that already knew Him as their savior, smiled, whispered the word *Amen* to express their thanks to the Lord.

The preacher smiled, raised his arms high and said, "Now, stand with me and sing that new song, *Shall We Gather at the River*. When they finished the song, the preacher said, "Now we'll be dismissed. But if you prayed that prayer and meant it with your whole heart, I want you to shake my hand and tell me you prayed and were saved today." He walked to the back of the room and stood by the door to shake hands with those that left. Reuben and Elly stood, turned to look at the back and were stirred as they saw many of the men, obviously telling the preacher they had prayed that prayer. Tears were streaming down the preacher's face, and many of those leaving were also in tears, tears of joy for having made that decision and saying that prayer.

As the crowd dispersed, the preacher saw Reuben, Elly, Estrella and Johnathan waiting and he walked to them. Reuben said, "Preacher Dyer, we would like you to come to lunch with us, would you do that?"

"Certainly. I'd be pleased to join you. Let me get my coat," he answered, stepping away to go to the back of the room to fetch his coat from the hook on the wall.

They were seated at a large circular table and the waitress was quick to take their order and pour their cups full of coffee. The preacher sat opposite Reuben and Elly, with Johnathan and Estrella to Elly's right. An empty chair was beside the preacher but full of coats and wraps. Reuben was lifting his cup to his lips and looked to the entrance to see a familiar figure. He quickly lowered his cup, looked to Elly, "That's Maude! There, in the doorway. I'm going to say hello, see if she'll join us." He rose and started to the couple but saw them going to a table and followed. As they were seated, he stood to the side, looked at Maude and smiled, caught her eye and watched her expression change as she recognized him.

"Well, if it ain't the devil his own self!" she declared, smiling and motioning him closer. She reached up both arms for Reuben to give her a hug and looked around for Elly. When she spotted her, she motioned for her to come over.

Maude turned, nodded to her companion, and said, "Reuben, I would like you to meet my husband, Fergus Riley," she smiled as she nodded to her man. He stood and Reuben was a little taken aback, for the man was about half the size of Maude. No more than five and a half feet tall, weighing maybe ten stone, bald on top with a ring of thinning hair above his ears, very few teeth and a nose that seemed to touch his chin when he talked. Reuben extended his hand, shook with the man who said, "Pleased ta' meet'cha!" nodded to Elly, and sat down.

Maude smiled broadly, "He's muh man, an' I shore do love him!" She leaned closer and whispered, "An' he done struck it rich, so that helps!" and giggled as she sat back, smiling.

They started to say more, but another figure filled the doorway and Reuben frowned, "Wonder what he's doin' here?" as he looked at Sheriff Jack Sparks. "He's out of his jurisdiction up here," but the man spotted Reuben and started toward him.

"Glad I found you," he declared, waving a piece of paper before him. "The telegrapher got this in, thought you'd be at the hotel in Fairplay, but they said you'd come up here. So, I needed to come thisaway to see a fella, and volunteered to bring it!" He handed the paper to Reuben who accepted it, frowning. He unfolded it, quickly read it, lifted his eyebrows and took a deep breath as he looked at the sheriff, "You read this?"

"Of course. It weren't in no envelope, and I thought it might be important. So, there ya go!"

"Well, thanks sheriff. Would you like to join us for lunch?" he asked, nodding to the table with the preacher.

The sheriff recognized the preacher, nodded, and looked at Reuben, "Nah, he makes me uncomfortable." He shook his head and turned away, exiting the dining room without another word. Reuben chuckled, ushered Elly back to the table and after seating her, took his seat as well. He looked to the door, saw another familiar figure and motioned them over, watching as Levi escorted his wife, Precious, to their table. The preacher quickly set the coats on the window seat, fetched another chair and motioned for the two to be seated.

It was a pleasant time visiting and sharing memories, but each had to return to their usual duties that did not stop just because the day was Sunday. Reuben looked to Preacher Dyer, "And you promise to check on this young lady every chance you get?" nodding toward Estrella.

He smiled, nodding, "Every chance I get, and I will call on both of them to help me whenever I have meetings here!" he nodded in the direction of Estrella and Johnathan, who smiled back. He looked at Johnathan, "And you, young man, after you made that decision this morning, I will expect to see you in every service!"

Johnathan smiled, "Oh, I will be, preacher, I promise. I know I have much to learn and I'm anxious to get started."

"Good, good," answered the preacher, smiling. He looked to Reuben and Elly, "And I expect to see you the next time you're in our area, also!"

"You will, preacher," answered Reuben.

As they walked down the hall to their room, Elly asked, "And what did the telegram say?"

237

Reuben chuckled, opened the door and stepped in after Elly. As she sat in the chair, he sat on the edge of the bed, opened the telegram and read –

Marshals Grundy
  South Park, CO
  Trouble in eastern Colorado territory. Stages, wagons, freighters being attacked on Cherokee Trail, Overland Trail, Smoky Hill Trail. Arapaho, Cheyenne, Kiowa, and Sioux involved, but also Confederate partisans. Chivington knows I am sending you. Troops will help. Do what you can.
  Governor Evans
  Colorado Territory

"So, that means we're goin' east?" asked Elly, a somber expression painting her face.

"I reckon," answered Reuben, lifting his foot to take off his boots. They would need to change to traveling clothes for this trip.

TAKE A LOOK AT ROCKY MOUNTAIN SAINT: THE COMPLETE CHRISTIAN MOUNTAIN MAN SERIES

Best-selling western author B.N. Rundell takes you on a journey through the wilderness in this complete 14-book mountain man saga!

Holding on to the dream of living in the Rocky Mountains that Tatum shared with his father, he begins his journey—a journey that takes him through the lands of the Osage and Kiowa and ultimately to the land of the Comanche. Now he has a family, and the wilderness makes many demands on anyone that tries to master the mountains…

"Rundell's Rocky Mountain Saint series is marvelous and inspiring." – **Reader**

Follow Tate Saint, man of the mountains, on his journey from boyhood to manhood where he faces everything from the wilds of the wilderness to forces of nature and historic wars.

Rocky Mountain Saint: The Complete Series includes – Journey to Jeopardy, Frontier Freedom, Wilderness Wanderin', Mountain Massacre, Timberline Trail, Pathfinder Peril, Wapiti Widow, Vengeance Valley, Renegade Rampage, Buffalo Brigade, Territory Tyranny, Winter Waifs, Mescalero Madness and Dine' Defiance.

AVAILABLE NOW

ABOUT THE AUTHOR

Born and raised in Colorado into a family of ranchers and cowboys, **B.N. Rundell** is the youngest of seven sons. Juggling bull riding, skiing, and high school, graduation was a launching pad for a hitch in the Army Paratroopers. After the army, he finished his college education in Springfield, MO, and together with his wife and growing family, entered the ministry as a Baptist preacher.

Together, B.N. and Dawn raised four girls that are now married and have made them proud grandparents. With many years as a successful pastor and educator, he retired from the ministry and followed in the footsteps of his entrepreneurial father and started a successful insurance agency, which is now in the hands of his trusted nephew. He has also been a successful audiobook narrator and has recorded many books for several award-winning authors. Now finally realizing his life-long dream, B.N. has turned his efforts to writing a variety of books, from children's picture books and young adult adventure books, to the historical fiction and western genres which are his first love.

Printed in Great Britain
by Amazon